You Can Never Find a Rickshaw When It Monsoons

THE WORLD ON ONE CARTOON A DAY

by MO WILLEMS

Foreword by Dave Barry

Hyperion Paperbacks/New York

My thanks to the world, including my parents
(to whom this book is dedicated) for giving me
both this trip and the travel bug that allowed
me to enjoy it

Text and illustrations copyright © 2006 by Mo Willems

Foreword copyright © 2006 by Dave Barry

First Edition

1 3 5 7 9 10 8 6 4 2

Library of Congress Cataloging-in-Publication Data

Willems, Mo.

You can never find a rickshaw when it monsoons: The world on one cartoon a day/by Mo Willems.
—1st pbk. ed. p. cm.

ISBN 0-7868-3747-0 (alk. paper)

1. Willems, Mo—Travel—Juvenile literature. 2. Willems, Mo—Diaries—Juvenile literature. 3. Authors,
American—21st century—Diaries—Juvenile literature. 4. Americans—Foreign countries—Juvenile
literature. 5. Voyages and travels—Juvenile literature. I. Title.

PS3623.I555ZA772006

818'.603—dc22

2005052722

Visit www.hyperionteens.com

FOREWORD

The first time I went abroad was in the mid-1970s, on a package tour run by TWA.[1] There were about three dozen of us on the tour, and we all had bought new sneakers. To make absolutely sure that there was no possible way that we could be mistaken for anything other than American tourists, we *also* were issued plastic shoulder bags the color of stop signs, with "TWA" on the sides.

The tour took us to four cities: London, France, Rome, and Vienna. In each city, a uniformed TWA guide met us at the airport and put us on a bus,[2] which took us to the official TWA-tour-affiliated hotel. Then we toured the city by bus, stopping at famous sights such as Big Ben and the Eiffel Tower, where we were allowed to briefly get off the bus so we could take photographs of ourselves standing in front of these sights, thereby documenting that we had seen them.

We also toured the countryside and stopped at—this is a very conservative estimate—every cathedral on the planet Earth. At each cathedral, the guide would point out interesting elements of the architecture, especially flying buttresses. My personal fascination with flying buttresses waned pretty quickly, but the tour guides found all of them to be absolutely riveting, and would not allow a single buttress to go unremarked.

The bus also took us to official TWA-tour-affiliated souvenir stores, where we could buy authentic *tchotchkes*,[3] and at night we went to official TWA-tour-affiliated restaurants, where we could choose from two, or sometimes even one, authentic entrees.

By the end of our two-week trip to four of the great cities of Europe, every person on the tour had a deeper understanding of, and appreciation

---

[1] For you younger readers: TWA is a now-defunct airline that was started by Leonardo DiCaprio.

[2] We always sat in the same seats. One time, one couple got crazy and sat in the seats that had been previously claimed by another couple, and there was nearly a fistfight.

[3] Yiddish for "crap."

for, the other people on the tour. This was inevitable, given all the hours we spent together on the bus. Some of us even exchanged addresses and phone numbers and promised to stay in touch, although of course we didn't. I've forgotten the other people on the tour, except for the one elderly stroke victim who had some kind of seizure when they heaved him into a rowboat during our group tour of the World-Famous Blue Grotto on the island of Capri.[4]

So what are my strongest and fondest memories of this, my first trip abroad? Not the buttresses, that's for sure. No, the moments that remain most vividly lodged in brain lobes of my mind are the experiences I had on those too-rare and too-brief occasions when we were off the bus and on our own, and found ourselves face-to-face with the true essence of European culture, by which I mean: toilets.

Back in the 1970s, Europe was still using the plumbing system originally installed by ancient Romans, and I vividly recall, more than once, descending into some dank, dark "restroom," where it was not easy to tell how to use the toilet, or for that matter where the actual toilet was. There was a very real danger that you would mess up and pee on a buttress. And to make the experience more unnerving, the men's toilets were often haunted, Gollum-style, by women attendants of the female gender, whose sole function, apparently, was to collect tips, a job that left them with no time for cleaning the toilets, as evidenced by the presence of carnivorous bacteria the size of Doberman pinschers.

I also vividly remember my attempts to use the municipal bus system in Rome, where I got onto a bus that I believed—because the route map said so—was going to take me to Point A, but which in fact went to a completely different place—Point R, maybe, or even Point Z—because (as was explained to me by a friendly Italian person who spoke some English[5]) the bus driver, for personal reasons, preferred to go to a different destination, and was not going to be confined by some rigid route map.

---

[4] If you are ever forced to choose between undergoing brain surgery with a blunt hoe or touring the World-Famous Blue Grotto, choose the surgery. I am serious.

[5] This pretty much describes all Italians.

Fortunately the trip was free, because (as also explained by the friendly Italian) the bus's fare machine was designed to accept only a certain kind of coin, but this coin was not available, because corrupt Italian politicians[6] had diverted the coins, via some scandalous scheme, to a company that was using them to make watches,[7] so it was physically impossible to pay to ride the bus, which seemed to be fine with everybody.

So I wound up getting thoroughly lost in Rome, miles from my destination. But the price was right, and I remember that trip better than any I took on the official TWA-tour bus.

I've done a lot more traveling since that trip, and I've learned that this is generally true: you of course want to see the famous sights, but in the end what you remember best about traveling to a new place is what you did not already know you would find there: the quirky, the unexpected, the weird, the scary. That's what sticks with you.

Which brings me (finally) to Mo Willems's wonderful book. In 1990, Mo traveled around the world, but he was definitely not on an official guided tour. His tour was as unofficial and unguided and random as humanly possible, and thus it was jam-packed with what I will call—and I mean this in a good way—toilet moments. Fortunately for us, Mo is ideally suited to capture those moments. He's a perceptive artist with a keen eye for the bizarre scene, the poignant detail, the amusing moment; he's also a very shrewd and very funny writer. ("I love dogs," he notes, "but not because they're smart.")

So what you have in your hands is a series of memorable moments, woven together into a fascinating, unpredictable voyage around the world, led by a highly entertaining guide. Enjoy the trip: you will not encounter a single buttress.

Dave Barry
Miami, Florida

[6] This may be redundant.

[7] I swear this is what the friendly Italian told me.

INTRODUCTION

There's this expression that goes, "It's a small world after all." Well, after a year tramping across the globe by plane, train, bus, boat, foot, and thumb, let me just say that it is, in fact, a very large world. To give you an idea of how big it truly is, try to imagine an abstract space fifteen football fields long by twenty-five football fields wide.

The world is much bigger than that.

Immediately after graduating from NYU in 1990, I packed a small backpack and set off to discover just how big the world was. Why bother, especially when a good sampling of the world had conveniently deposited itself in my New York City neighborhood? Good question. Perhaps in order to "expand my horizons," or to see if people really are the same wherever you go.[1] These sound like good reasons—better than the real one: I simply wasn't ready to start an uncertain career in animation,[2] and a big trip around the world seemed like a plausible way to save face.

This is not to say that the idea came out of the blue. I was reared in a traveling family. As a young man, my Dutch father had spent several months in Persia, the Middle East, and Africa. When I was growing up in New Orleans, my family returned to Holland whenever my parents' bank account allowed. At fifteen, I walked across France with my father, retracing Napoleon's triumphant escape from Elba as he reestablished his emperorship. The 700-mile trek not only taught me the benefits of a steely resolve and light backpack, but upon my return my parents deemed me ready for the Holy Grail of teenage-dom: a driver's license. Maybe a trip around the world at twenty-two would qualify me for some sort of "adulthood license"? Regardless, I'd already told everyone I was going to circumnavigate the globe from west to east like a baseball thrown by Bugs Bunny, so I kinda had to.

---

[1] Fortunately, they're not. The trip would have been a bore if everyone really had been the same.

[2] My parents were unwise enough to invest in my obtaining an animation degree, so I felt an obligation to at least try to become an animator.

With minimal preparation,[3] I booked a one-way ticket to London and eased into the journey, starting off on the well-worn "Summer in Europe" path with a college buddy, visiting England (where I had spent a summer a few years earlier as an aspiring stand-up comic), Holland (a nation littered with my relatives), and France (where an ex-girlfriend was living for the summer) before tackling more challenging regions. By the end of the summer, I'd spent almost a month in Turkey and had fallen in love with deserts and the odd quietude of touring solo.

Come fall, my pace slowed as the locales became more alien and interesting. My sideburns began their precipitous drop toward my shoulders; my pants became patched with bits of local cloth; and I had jettisoned the majority of my belongings. In short, I was becoming a Traveler.[4]

If you're taking a two-week holiday, it's best to use your time wisely. But for someone who's on the road for six, nine, twelve months, or longer,[5] time warps as the days blend in and out of each other. You may be constantly on the move,[6] but your social life becomes oddly static as you bump into the same people over distances of thousands of miles. You're one of a motley collection of eccentrics, misfits, and cute Nordic girls[7] attended to by wacky locals whose boardinghouses serve as flop pads, living rooms, and a source of banana pancakes[8] to the backpacking hordes.

Cast about in this sea of characters, I spent twelve months aimless and free to spend my days visiting the planet's great natural and architectural wonders, with only my sketch diary to ground me. Doodling every day was the ritual that held the trip together, gave it purpose, made it real. Fifteen years later, I'm grateful to have these sketches; they're my gateway to

---

[3] My map of the world was an old poster from a 1960s feature in *LIFE* magazine, entitled "Communism: Know Your Enemy."

[4] Travelers are supposed to disdain Tourists, who visit the exact same sites for the exact same reasons, but commit the unforgivable sin of purchasing T-shirts to prove they've been there.

[5] I met countless people who'd been on the road for ages, including a cyclist who'd spent twenty-six (count 'em twenty-six) years cycling through every country on the planet. He told me with a straight face that he planned to return to his home and sleep in his childhood bed in another year or two.

[6] The longest I spent in one place was two weeks in a dollar-a-night shack in Kathmandu.

[7] Very cute Nordic girls.

[8] Access to great banana pancakes must be an article of the Geneva Convention. I have yet to visit a region, no matter how remote, whose boardinghouses did not serve them.

understanding the weird guy who occupied my skinny body back then.

It's not only I who was different fifteen years ago; the world was. 1990–91 corresponded with the end of the Cold War. Germany was on the cusp of reunification, while Czechoslovakia and Yugoslavia were on the verge of breaking up. I entered Turkey just as Iraq invaded Kuwait,[9] which altered the Turks' attitude toward my American self.[10]

It can be disconcerting meeting up with your younger self.

The list goes on: Egypt's Fundamentalists condemning Western tourists, Pakistan's preelection strikes and disturbances,[11] India awash in strikes and riots,[12] Kathmandu filled with large democracy protests and a Marxist insurgency. I arrived in Bangladesh the day of a big revolt, and the Chinese were more wary of me than they had been in my previous visit a year earlier.[13]

Still, political upheaval had its advantages. One night, I arrived at the posh apartment of some family friends in Singapore to discover two

[9] Starting a standoff that has yet to be resolved as of this writing.

[10] Some wanted the U.S. to kick Saddam's butt, some wanted to kick mine.

[11] This was back when Pakistan was a democracy.

[12] About everything, from religion to who got into the good colleges.

[13] Of course, the Tiananmen Square Massacre had occurred between my first and second visit, and few locals wanted to be suspected of being too friendly to "outside influences."

things: I was crashing a large, fancy dinner party, and I smelled terrible. The guests tried to be polite as they surveyed the skinny, stinky, disheveled mess before them, but it's hard to be polite while you're holding your nose and hacking. Just then, CNN began broadcasting live war footage from Kuwait, and everyone ran to the television, allowing me to slink off to the bathroom for a long-overdue shower.

Much like my ambling trip, there was no grand scheme to the cartoons I drew as I traveled. The daily sketch might not have been the most relevant or even funny event of the day. It was simply the one that stood out the most when I sat down in the evening and pulled out my paper, ink, and pens.[14] Each drawing was made on or very near to the day it depicts, without the benefit of preliminary sketches, art-supply stores, or a spell-checker. If the contemporary annotations don't always give context to the drawings, hopefully they'll include a few cool stories.

I don't pretend to have understood (or now understand) all of my experiences, even though I tried to. Like a rock tossed across the Mississippi River, I merely skimmed the world, bouncing off places as far and as long as I could.

I hope the resulting cartoon diary will be a kick for you to flip through. It may give you a sense of the rhythm of extended travels; the mundane routine of transportation augmented by consistent physical and cultural shocks. It may even inspire you to pack up a few belongings and take a trip of your own. If you do, please don't forget your paper and pens.

Mo Willems
Brooklyn, New York

---

[14] For those who care, my supplies included a plastic ink-pot, B-2 and A-5 nibs, a cracked pen holder, a .35 technical pen, and a brush wrapped in an old bandana.

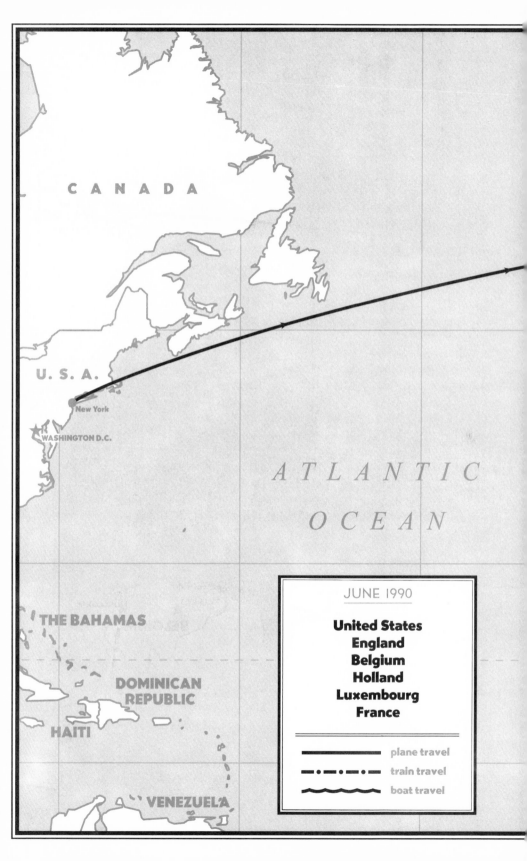

C A N A D A

U. S. A.

New York

WASHINGTON D.C.

A T L A N T I C

O C E A N

THE BAHAMAS

DOMINICAN
REPUBLIC

HAITI

VENEZUELA

JUNE 1990

United States
England
Belgium
Holland
Luxembourg
France

plane travel
train travel
boat travel

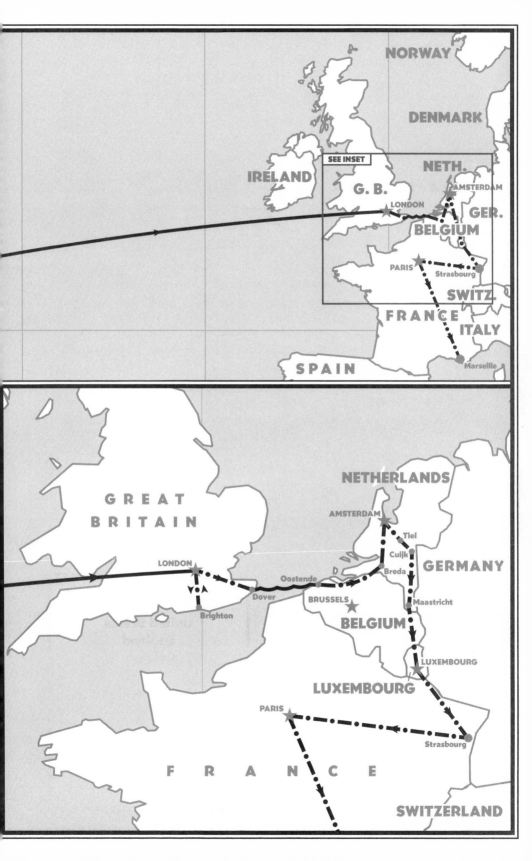

6/1 - young man tries to tell punks on the A-train to stop smoking (new york)

What better way to start an around-the-world trip than on the subway? Like the trip itself, the subway's cheap, makes all stops, and is chock-full of cross-cultural exchanges.

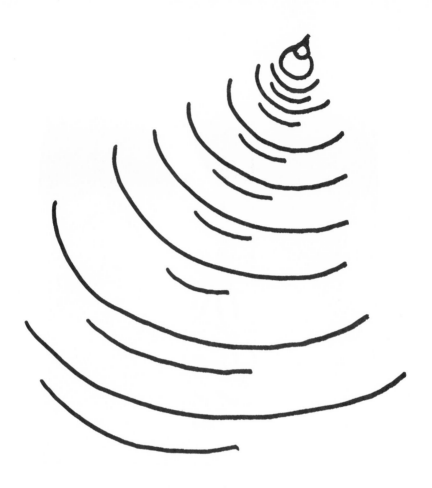

6/2 - duckling (finsbury park, london)

Having spent the previous few months busily getting ramped up for the big trip, I arrived in the U.K. only to discover that my friends were inconsiderate enough to have remained in the real world, where they had jobs. Suddenly, I found myself with absolutely nothing to do during the days except sit in the park and watch the world go by.

6/3 - I am no cook
(london)

. . . neither are the British. Only two days on the road and I missed my NYC diner breakfast specials.

6/4 – debate on the reasons for paying 50p to sit on a chair (st. james' park, london)

If I was going to have to pay a buck every time I sat down, I'd be broke before I hit Spain.

6/5 - boy rides the
bumper car with
no one to bump
(brighton, UK)

Okay, so it's not quite *Waiting for Godot*, but still . . .

6/6 - bad imitation of bad american food & batman (london)

The fact that **WIMPY BURGER** is a big chain in England still gives me the giggles.

6/7 - great men &
fallen men (victoria gardens,)
london

Back in the grand, old days of Imperial England, gentlemen dreamed of doing great things for Queen and Country so that history would memorialize them in statues for drunks to pee on.

Ye olde 2 5 watt Light Bulbs!

6/8 - lonely, bored
shopkeeper happy
to give directions
(covent garden, london)

England is such an expensive country, yet charmingly obscure shop(pe)s
somehow manage to stay open.

6/9 - drunken drama students (woodgreen, london)

Acting up, if not acting . . .

6/10 - punks' playtime
by playground (camden town,
london)

By 1990 punks were desperate to show they were as hard-core as their
parents had been in the 1970s.

6/11- football fans
in a pub (london)

It was a World Cup year, which inflamed great passion in the Brits. I'd been a bartender in a pub during the '86 Cup, and every evening, patrons would bring in photographs of their greatest moments of hooliganism.

That was mean of me, wasn't it? I was probably jealous that they wouldn't air-kiss a certain backpacker.

6/13 - soused aussie sings
(ferry, dover to oostende)

Perhaps they come standard with a third-class ticket, because never in my life have I taken a ferry trip that didn't include at least one drunken Australian guitar player.

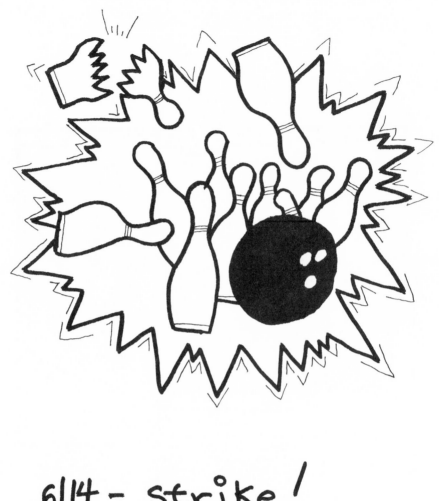

6/14 - strike!
(breda-holland)

Back in the early '60s my father was the manager of the first bowling alley in Holland. It was there that he met my mother. The story goes that he informed my mother's date that his bowling stank. The date left in a huff, so my father continued bowling the set with my flummoxed mother. I know, I know: weird. Even so, I always make it a point to bowl a set when visiting Holland.

6/15 - friday 3:30 pm &
the kids take over
the center of town
(breda, holland)

Besides having some interesting churches and fortresses, Breda boasts a most active Dutch bar scene. Cafés fill early and empty late with patrons ranging in age from 16 to 96.

Liberal and hip, Amsterdam was a squatters' paradise where you could complain to the government for not supplying sufficient electricity and heat to your illegal (and free) abode. My second cousin and her pals merrily took advantage of this, living the hipsters' subsidized dream life.

6/17 - my extended family (tiel, holland)

The undisputed boss of our large Catholic family, my grandmother (or Oma) was large in every way possible. She would plop her huge breasts on the table before sitting down, take a gargantuan breath, and proceed to yap nonstop for hours on end. The rest of the family could only grab their seats and hold on for dear life, waiting for this force of nature to be spent. It was, invariably, a long wait.

6/18 dante's inferno.
being force-fed by
your grandmother
(cuijk, holland)

She insisted on stuffing everyone within waddling distance.

6/19 - 8:50 am (cuijk, holland)

Oma was incorrigible (although now that I'm a father it's funny that being woken at 8:50 in the morning ever seemed cruel and unusual). Unfortunately, this day did not go Oma's way at all. She'd been under the misconception that my spending a year traveling around the world would entail ten months of being force-fed by her in a tiny suburban apartment followed by a quick weekend jaunt to, say, Paris, before returning to her sizable bosom. When I took leave that afternoon, the room quickly filled with outsized tears.

6/20 - street performer
or very sad man?

As I traveled, I met a great number of people who eked out a living performing as they bounced around from town to town. While they tended to be contemptuous of normal people, with their mortgages and families, these vagabonds seldom seemed happy with their lot.

6/21 - the waiter & the calculator
(luxembourg)

(* 100 - 30 = 70)

Luxembourg, which I imagined to be a hilly, fairy-tale land, was a disappoint-ment. Hilly it was, but otherwise the town was dank, gray, and uninviting. Perhaps because its banking industry serves as a global money-laundering facility, the locals distrust outsiders taking pictures or asking questions. Not everyone in Luxemburg could keep a ledger, though.

6/22 - the dog who
slobbered on my
book & his owner
(strasbourg, france)

Both of them seemed to like my drawings. Good thing I used waterproof ink.

1. policeman
2. bus driver
3. american tourist
4. paris citizen
5. metro rider
6. bohemian

6/23 - some of the facial hair to be seen (strasbourg, paris, france)

Now facial hair is all the rage, but in 1990 New York, sideburns were far-out, and a goatee, radical. These guys' whiskers spoke volumes about their owners.

6/24 - wine, cheese, beer, bread, cigarettes, & chocolate (paris, france)

Ah, the romantic French lifestyle; living in an attic flat, drinking wine, smoking, and lazily discussing philosophy. I never met any Frenchmen who did that, but my Yankee buddies who were spending the year there had the drill down to perfection.

6/25 - night traffic
(paris, france)

Paris's grand avenues are filled with hordes of zooming cars, the ultimate challenge to a jaywalking New Yorker.

6/26 - Park employee
requests the patrons
Keep off the grass
(paris, france)

Lesson learned. Every city has different hot-button issues.

6/27 - dog who confused
a cement flowerpot
with food (paris, france)

I love dogs, but not because they're smart.

6/28 - children & statues
(paris, france)

In England, statues' main function seemed to be propping up drunks (see 6/7), but the French had a more healthy disrespect for public art; they were just looking for climb-ability.

6/29-night train
(paris to marseille, France)

Being a sucker for trains makes the night train exhausting: I never get any sleep, from staring out the window all night long.

6/30 - bathers & gold diggers
(marseille, France)

The topless beaches of the Côte d'Azur are apparently alluring enough to make people drop their watches into the sea. Those women concerned about sunburned breasts would do better to swim in Malaysia (see 1/7).

ADMITTED
U. S. CUSTOMS
U. S. IMMIGRATION
JFK AIRPORT

U. DATE
NEW YORK, N.Y.
JUN 07

ADMITTED
UNTIL

-2 JUN 1990
GATWICK

LEAVE TO ENTER FOR SIX MONTHS
EMPLOYMENT PROHIBITED

DIRECCION DE ESTADO
-FRONTERAS-
C. 7. 90   0 0
F ENTRAD
YUSTAPUESTO

LEAVE TO ENTER FOR SIX MONTHS
EMPLOYMENT PROHIBITED.

BELGIË · U
HAVEN OOSTENDE
10 - 1 - 1989
14
ZEEVAARTPOLITIE

IMMIGRATION OFFICER
(3)   *
-2 JAN 1989
HEATHROW (3)

LEAVE TO ENTER FOR SIX MONTHS
EMPLOYMENT PROHIBITED

IMMIGRATION OFFICER
*   (45)   *
10 JAN 1989
DOVER (W)

BELGIË · U
HAVEN OOSTENDE
04 - 1 - 1989
ZEEVAARTPOLITIE

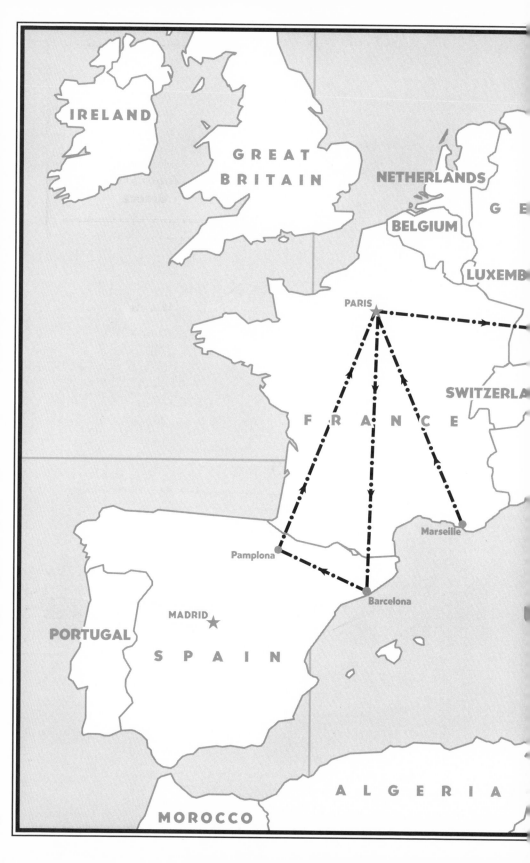

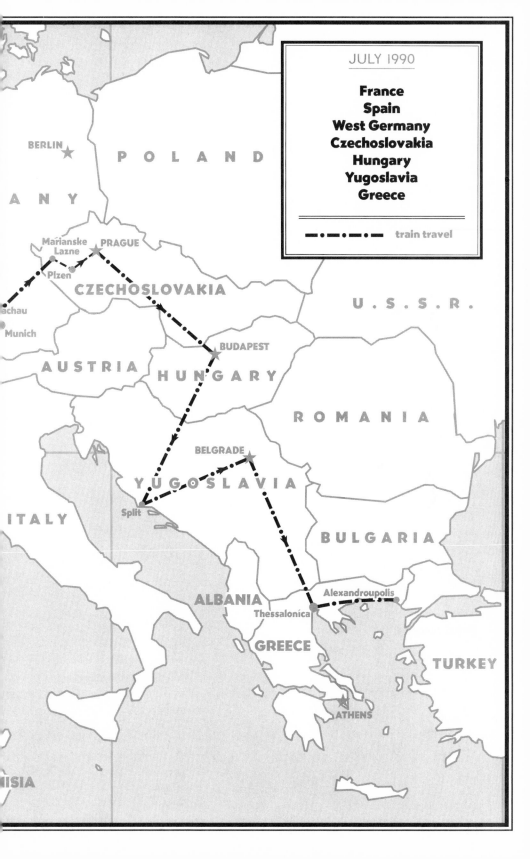

JULY 1990

France
Spain
West Germany
Czechoslovakia
Hungary
Yugoslavia
Greece

■—·—■—·—■—·—·— train travel

BERLIN ★

P O L A N D

ANY

Marianske Lazne
Plzen
PRAGUE
CZECHOSLOVAKIA

achau

Munich

U . S . S . R .

A U S T R I A

BUDAPEST

H U N G A R Y

R O M A N I A

BELGRADE

Y U G O S L A V I A

Split

ITALY

B U L G A R I A

ALBANIA

Alexandroupolis

Thessalonica

GREECE

TURKEY

ATHENS

NISIA

7/01 - boy who sleeps in a suit (marseille, france)

It was in a ramshackle old mansion that had been converted into a ramshackle youth hostel that I made contact with my first of the "really weird backpackers," a glorious subset of characters that make traveling much more interesting. This guy planned to spend the summer wearing his suit on the beach (he carried his towel in a briefcase).

7/02 - man kicks pigeon
(barcelona, spain)

Perhaps here begins my affinity with pigeons. . . .

4/03- old enough to smoke, young enough to play hide-&-seek (barcelona, spain)

One disadvantage of being a kid who chain-smokes while playing hide-and-seek: the smoke always gives you away. . . .

7/4 -evening street music (pamplona, spain)

Having hooked up with a buddy from college, we picked up a few other folks we met in Barcelona and quickly headed to Pamplona, eager to check out the annual Running of the Bulls. Arriving a day early (to snag the best part of the park to sleep), I managed to spend the afternoon marching around the romantic, sleepy town. All that would change by the time we woke up in the park the next morning.

7/05 – the kids also drink the champagne
(festival san fermin, pamplona, spain)

The festival San Fermin, or Running of the Bulls, is one of the most riotous, wild events I've experienced. Like Mardi Gras revelers on steroids, locals and tourists alike go all out for this one. The city's park becomes an open-air motel, its fountains become showers, and certain squares transform into national homesteads. The wildest, as usual, was the Australian section, where Aussie boys got tanked, climbed as high as they could, and plummeted to the ground, hoping someone would catch them. Even with the city's removal of statuary (which is Australian for "diving boards"), some of the boys managed to scale the walls of the bars and apartment buildings. Other quarters remained fiercely local and religious in their festivities. All this occurred before they let the bulls loose on the streets.

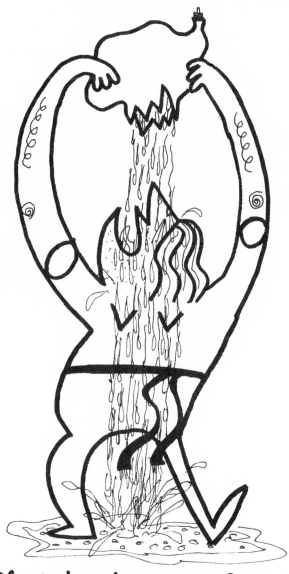

7/06 - what to do if your pigskin breaks
(festival san fermin, pamplona, spain)

The party is so unrelenting, everyone's traditional white shirts and pants are quickly doused in enough wine to make them match their red sashes.

7/07 — we cheer the bulls
(festival san fermin, pamplona, spain)

The best deal for the halfway sane partier is to forego the actual (and very dangerous) early-morning running of the bulls and head right for the bull-ring. Once safely sitting in the arena, you can watch as "brave" Aussies, local boys, and assorted blithering idiots dash into the ring inches ahead of an angry herd of stampeding bulls. Once everyone is in, the next forty minutes are spent watching the humans jump around, trying to catch the attention of the riotous crowd as bulls randomly deck them from behind. It's like a demolition derby with people, and unlike the fights in the afternoons, it's free, and the bulls never lose.

7/08 - still life
(festival san fermín, pamplona, spain)

Did I mention that the party was unrelenting?

7/09- morning: some try to walk their dogs, some try to walk (festival san fermin, pamplona, Spain)

By this time the locals were pretty much over the whole thing. . . .

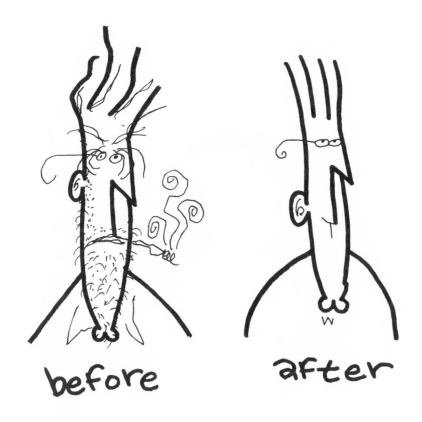

before

after

7/10 - paris, france (via train
pamplona → san sebastian → hendaye →
paris)

The shower I took after stumbling out of Pamplona was the best I have ever taken.

7/11- bank teller who changes money and suggests cold remedies
(paris, france)

This bank teller was so sweet and concerned about my health, I couldn't tell her that my cold was the product of sleeping in a Spanish park and partying too much for a week.

7/12- beer to man:
proportional sizes
[actual size] (train: munich, w. germany)

still

Lots of history, lovely architecture, but Munich sells itself on its beer.

7/13 - american students discuss the problems with today's sorority pledges
(dachau, w.germany)

Seeing this banal conversation take place inside a former concentration camp was by far the most shocking event of my trip.

7/14 - entropy & antiquity
(mariánské,
czechoslovakia)

Mariánské Lánzě is a lovely old spa town nestled in the Czech woods. It's also lot of fun to say over and over again.

7/15 - the woods
(mariánské Lánzě, czechoslovakia)

Dense and foreboding, these are the woods where a Little Red Riding Hood could easily run into a Big Bad Wolf.

7/16 - directions to the camping, a sample
(plzeň, Czechoslovakia)

When we finally reached the camping ground (which was just around the corner), I met a nice, hapless Aussie who'd rented a cabin on the grounds. That night he left his only sneakers outside the shack and awoke the next morning to discover they'd been taken. A few days later, in Prague, I ran into the guy; he was wearing the ugliest shoes ever made. It turns out that he had had to walk barefoot back into town searching for shoes. Unfortunately, the one shoe store in town had a strict policy: "No Shoes No Service." His only recourse was to have a shoe-wearing local go into the store and buy a pair for him and keep the change. The local must have kept a lot of change by the look of those shoes.

7/17 - czech fashion
(plzeň, czechoslovakia)

With the collapse of communism, the American flag was more popular abroad than at home. Seems like a long time ago.

7/18 - a gallery of heroes
(a beer hall, prague, czechoslovakia)

Stalin, Brezhnev, and Gorbachev (but not the lady in the calendar) had been plastered on the bar walls during the Czech's communist era. After the Velvet Revolution, they retained their place of honor, but were transformed into an ironic joke that everyone was now free to laugh at.

7/19 - youth hangout

(Karlöv most bridge, prague,
CZechoslovakia

Prague at the time was hyped as the new Paris, a place for artists to hang out on the cheap.

7/20- old war songs
(prague, czechoslovakia)

This old warrior didn't miss a beat, even while missing two fingers.

7/21 - the multi-headed
beast of train ticket
bureaucracy (prague,
czechoslovakia)

I was sent all the way across town three times to various departments, to obtain the correct obscure stamps that would allow me to board a train (apparently someone had forgotten to inform the rail department that communism was over). This was only the first of many similar trials in a multicontinental battle to buy a train ticket. In China you had to buy your ticket from the correct seller; in India a bus ticket consisted of over a hundred scraps of paper in your hand.

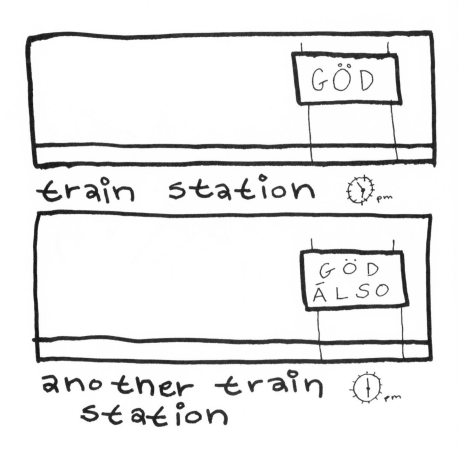

train station 🕐 pm

another train 🕐 pm
station

7/2² - on the way
to budapest
(hungary)

Honest to Göd.

7/23 - accommodation hustlers (budapest, hungary)
outside of american express office

Now that "free enterprise" was the all the rage in Eastern Europe, every-one was eager to meet rubes with dollars.

7/24 - selling folk goods
in the metro station
(budapest, hungary)

"Free enterprise" had its costs as well.

7/25 - mild-mannered
ma'am on train
(budapest, hungary to Zagreb, yugoslavia)

And she flipped through the magazine, expressionless—like it was required reading.

7/26 - alice cooper &
abba (train:
Zagreb → split, yugoslavia)

Free, young, and punk, these kids dreamed of seeing Alice Cooper and ABBA together in concert. Come to think of it, so do I.

7/27 - the ruins & the ruiners (split, yugoslavia)

How wrong I was. It was the subsequent war that actually ruined the town. Far from being tawdry, those tourists' pictures are some of the only proof of the ancient civilizations that flourished in the former Yugoslavia; now it's mostly rubble.

7/28 - train-sleeping
position (split →
beograd, yugoslavia

The next several days would be spent on slow-moving trains vaguely lumbering toward Turkey. It took a while to figure out this relatively comfortable position.

7/29- cleaning lady's
reaction to those who
put their feet on the seats
(train: beograd, yugoslavia → thessalonica, greece)

My relatively comfortable position was not appreciated, however.

7/30 - dirty old greek
man & australian
transcend language
barriers (train: thessalonica →
alexandroupolis, greece)

Travel! Meet new people and talk about boobs!

7/31- store window
(alexandroupolis, greece)

To be honest, some of those cute, pink, fluffy, stuffed animals deserved to be harpooned. Think of it as one-stop shopping.

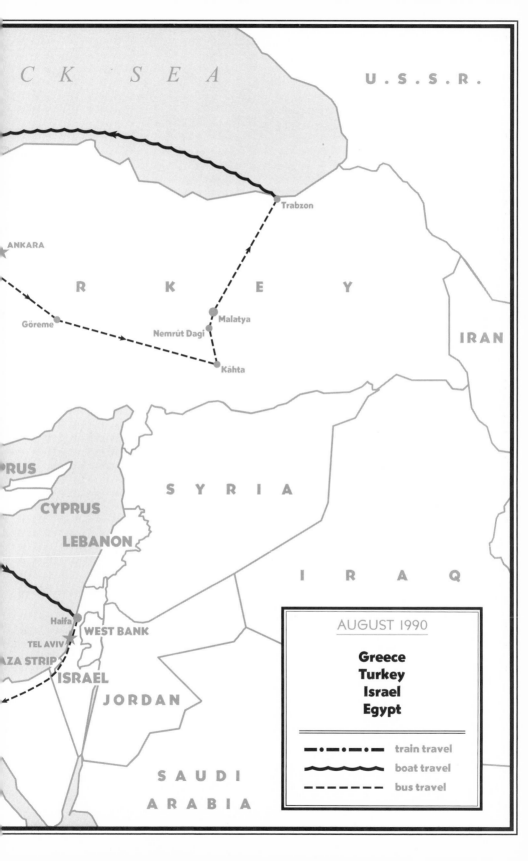

C K · S E A

U.S.S.R.

Trabzon

ANKARA

R   K   E   Y

Göreme
Nemrût Dagi   Malatya

IRAN

Kâhta

RUS

CYPRUS

LEBANON

S Y R I A

I R A Q

Haifa
WEST BANK
TEL AVIV
AZA STRIP
ISRAEL
JORDAN

SAUDI

ARABIA

8/01 - meeting of the portable & static water salesmen (istanbul, turkey)

Those water carriers signaled that I'd entered a different culture. (Sure, guys hawk water in Central Park during the summer, but without the cool, traditional outfits.) The carrier had the advantage of being able to get to the crowds, but the static guy's back didn't hurt as much.

air

fire

earth

water

8/02 - water pipe as the
four elements
(ali pashar's bazaar,
istanbul, turkey)

I quickly became enraptured with the *shesha* (a water pipe distinct from a Pakistani hookah) with my first experience at a small touristic coffeehouse. Contrary to its druggy image in the States, puffing on the tobacco-filled *shesha* is a rather dull, middle-aged pastime, best enjoyed with a game of dominoes. The Turks used a sort of pre-rolled cigar, which was, frankly, gross. Within a month I would be in Egypt, where I would become a devotee of the local, loose, honey-soaked tobacco. The shape of the water pipe is supposed to evoke a woman's curves.

8/03 - birthday costume?*
(istanbul, turkey)

* 8/06 - this is the traditional costume for the
CIRCUMCISION ceremony.

Three years later, I was lucky enough to witness a traditional circumcision ceremony in Tunisia. A big neighborhood party filled with fun, food, and highly infectious religious chanting, the entire event takes almost a week, during which time a boy is primped, spoiled, and generally made to feel like a prince (without being informed of his impending snippage). The party reaches a fever pitch on the final evening as the boy (aged anywhere from three to twelve) is whisked upstairs for the operation (an event witnessed by all the men, who stand around with their hands casually protecting their crotches). When the deed in done, a ceramic jug filled with candy is shattered in the central courtyard, the women cluck ecstatically, and the boy tries to put on a brave face. A post-snip boy continues to wear his princely, Disneyfied costume for a few days; his miserable expression and reluctance to sit down confirming his circumcision to all.

8/04 - Both look & are looked at.

(göreme, turkey)

Strikingly beautiful and hauntingly weird, Göreme is the center of a region of hill-and-cave complexes where some of the first Christians burrowed to avoid persecution. The soft rock outcroppings are filled with winding underground passages, covered in eccentric, primitive iconostases. Add a traditional Turkish Muslim population and busloads of tourists jetted in for the day, and you get one of the freakiest places I'd ever been to. I couldn't get enough of it.

8/05 - how to read the carpets & kilims
(göreme, turkey)

My fascination with the kilim was born while chatting with this English lit. major/carpet seller in a small stall on the outskirts of town. He attended to the occasional busloads of tourists with subtle disdain (because they were only interested in carpets that matched their furniture back home and missed the stories woven into every piece). Between buses, we sat and drank sweet tea while he wove tales about the various designs. The best afternoon of the trip.

8/06- pension owner's
late-night saz concert
(göreme, turkey)

This dude performed traditional romantic ballads with fluctuating passion.
Somehow his renditions were especially heartfelt when cute, Western girls
were in his impromptu audience.

8/07 – getting out of
the bus. each says his
Pension is better
       (kahta, turkey)

Like much of the world, Turkey was filled with eager entrepreneurs, desperate for my meager supply of dollars.

8/08 – after 3½ hours
of trekking, realizing you've
Scaled the wrong mountain
(not quite nemrut dagi, turkey)

Nemrut Dagi features the glorious ruins of a mysterious cult (one that the locals thought might be Christian because of all the Westerners who now flock to it). The only way to truly experience the majesty of the broken statues (according to my travel buddy) was to scale the mountain and see the sight at sunset. Luckily, after we realized we'd scaled the wrong summit, we managed to hitch a ride up the correct mountain. The punch line: I developed a hernia on the climb that plagued me in Nepal (see 11/10) and for the next ten years.

8/09 - mother whose son is leaving for the army (bus station, malatya, turkey)

Thanks to the Turkish-Kurdish conflict, conscription to the army did not guarantee a soldier would return after his tour. We would hear a lot more about this from the local Kurds we met at cafés and such.

8/10 - trying to learn turkish
card game (trabzon, turkey)

I'm a lousy gambler and he knew it.

8/11- priceless art devalued
(sumela monastery, turkey)

Some of the walls in Turkey bear the mark of the ideas that have passed through the country over the ages: icons of Christ, Islam's rules against drawing human faces (for fear of idol worship), and American tourists' quest for some kind of fame.

8/12 - two women, one
facing east, one facing
west (trabzon, turkey)

Now only more so.

8/13 – Kurdish radical
intent on publicizing
his plight & sending
his son to fight
(trabzon, turkey)

Today, most Americans have some knowledge of the Kurds and their political aspirations; fifteen years ago it wasn't a subject for the nightly news. So, many men were eager to convince passing tourists of the justice of their cause.

8/14- boy pours my cola
For me (trabzon, turkey)

A perfect lazy day.

8/15 - turkish bath
(trabzon, turkey)

The *hammam* is a fantastically relaxing cornerstone of Turkish life. After a thorough beating, scrubbing, and bending, the bath's clientele are wrapped in thin towels and left to read, puff on their *sheshas*, or stare blankly in blissful stupor.

8/16 - some people are better off dressed
(boat from trabzon → istanbul via black sea)

Speaking of a blissful stupor . . . This guy was the husband of a German lady who rated the relative worth of nations on the cleanliness of their toilets. Her advice for my travels was invaluable: all I had to do was follow the exact opposite of everything she said to find fun places to go.

8|17 - my tummy
(istanbul, turkey)

The perennial backpacker's battle, but as the year continued, I quickly bounced back from these bouts of stomach trouble.

8/18 - patriotic
paranoia pops up:
stuck between two
IRANIAN tourists
(post office, istanbul, turkey)

I shudder at the stupidity of my youth when I look at this sketch. These guys were quite happy to separate who I was from my government, but I was unwilling or unable to do the same for them. A wasted opportunity.

8/19 - museum guard
stationed next to
the video documentary
on a continuous loop
(istanbul, turkey)

I'd worked in a Soho gallery with a video loop when I was in college, so I had
great empathy for this guy.

8/20 - the government doctor (the mad quest for malaria pills, istanbul, turkey)

Ahh . . . silly national pride. Not having secured antimalarial pills in the States, I was eager to do so before I visited other nations where malaria could be a concern. Unfortunately, most Turkish doctors took my quest as an insult, angrily bellowing, "THERE IS NO MALARIA IN TURKEY!" Luckily, my mother was Honorary Consul for Holland back home, so after a few calls from the Dutch consulate, someone gave me some pills (powdered chemicals individually placed in tiny digestible wafer boxes), which proved helpful when I did become ill in Egypt.

8/21 - turkish bus
station (night bus: istanbul → selçuk, turkey)

Turkish bus stations were an attraction in and of themselves: raw, brightly lit islands in the middle of quiet, traditional neighborhoods. Australian backpackers couldn't get over how the biggest bus line, "Kamilz Koc," sounded like a dromedary's genitals. I never took one of their buses without encountering a few Aussies giggling in the back.

8/22- italian tourist poses as if he himself sculpted the ruin (Selçuk museum, turkey)

With the entire region strewn with ruins, it became all too easy to feel that everything you did was futile in the long run. At least, it did for me. But this guy felt an unnatural pride in monuments constructed by his great-grandparents.

8/23- the waiter who
wanted to make sure
my dinner was fine
(marmaris, turkey)

A nice guy, I guess. But there's no need to inquire about how each bite tasted.

8/24- sunbathers
soddenly showered
(Rhodes, greece)

The boat from Turkey to Israel only stopped on Rhodes long enough for me to get soaked.

DECK PASSENGERS ARE <u>NOT</u> ALLOWED TO USE THIS TOILET

8/25 - deck passenger
uses ~~that~~ ~~toilet~~
(boat Rhodes, greece →
Haifa, israel)

Third-class in this boat meant sitting on the roof with a loose tarp flapping over your head. You wanted toilets, you should have bought second-class tickets.

8/26 - things get out
of control at passport
control (haifa, israel)

Fun in the sun, indeed. While not as hard to enter as Canada (see 5/14,
5/16), this was not an easy border crossing.

8/27 — fun in the sun
(tel aviv beach, israel)

I entered Israel largely ignorant of the region's politics. But with intense animosity on both sides, there was little fun to be had in the suburban-esque Haifa.

8/28 - response after asking directions to the bus station (not the tel aviv bus station, israel)

Having heard fantastic things about Jerusalem, I resolved to visit that day, but after getting lost I discovered I'd missed that day's bus. Another was just leaving for Cairo, so I thought, What the heck? and took it.

8/29 - on the assumption that a tourist will buy anything, an egyptian turns on the hard sell with women's underwear
(cairo, egypt)

The madness that was Cairo astounded me. Loud, dusty, dirty, filled to the brim with every sort of person from the Arab and African world hawking everything imaginable, the town was less of a melting pot than a boiling pot. I loved every minute of it.

8/30 - young men amused
by my silly clothes
(cairo, egypt)

The innocence and goodwill of this encounter would, sadly, be harder to achieve today.

8/31–the political discussion
(cairo, egypt)

A discussion isn't a discussion until some old-fashioned yelling, gesticulating, and occasional spitting takes place.

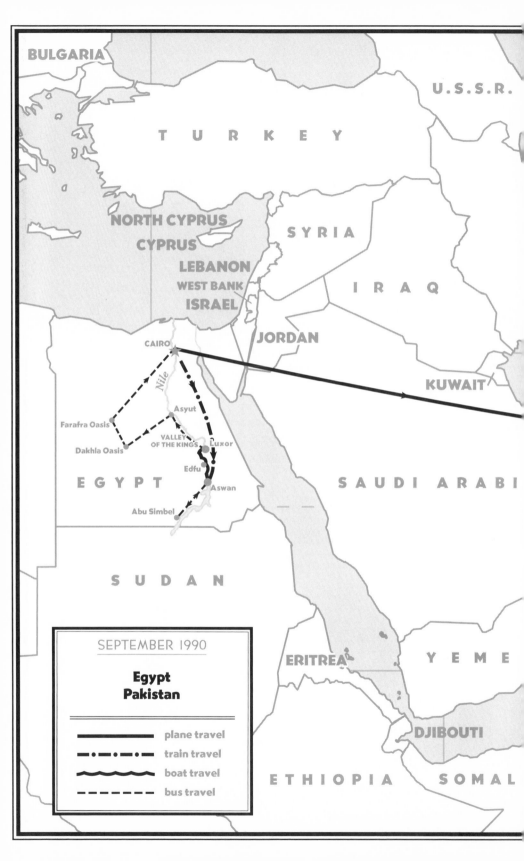

BULGARIA

U.S.S.R.

T U R K E Y

NORTH CYPRUS
CYPRUS
LEBANON
WEST BANK
ISRAEL

S Y R I A

I R A Q

JORDAN

KUWAIT

CAIRO

Nile

Asyut

Farafra Oasis

VALLEY
OF THE KINGS   Luxor

Dakhla Oasis

Edfu

E G Y P T

Aswan

SAUDI ARABI

Abu Simbel

S U D A N

ERITREA

Y E M E

DJIBOUTI

SEPTEMBER 1990

**Egypt
Pakistan**

——————— plane travel
— · — · — · — train travel
〜〜〜〜〜 boat travel
— — — — — bus travel

E T H I O P I A   SOMAL

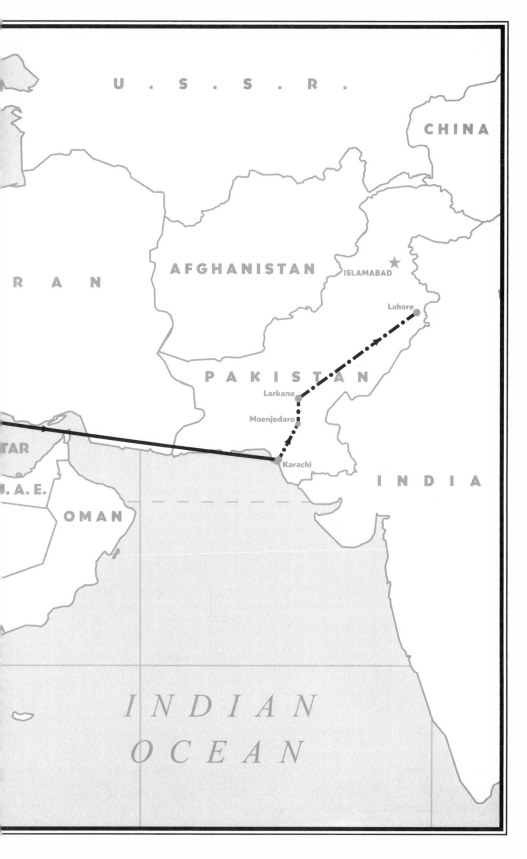

9/01 - the auto accident
(cairo, egypt)

those actually involved in the accident
are indicated by the arrows

This argument was being held in the middle of the street (consequently blocking all the road's traffic), so more and more people entered the fray in a counterintuitive attempt to speed things up.

9/02 - maternal instinct
aroused: being offered
food on the train
(cairo → aswan, egypt)

This kindness occurred along a train line that five years later was frequently interrupted by anti-Western snipers.

9/03 - bottles of water
consumed in the
heat of aswan
(aswan, egypt)

The remarkably intense heat is difficult for outsiders to bear. The local head wraps prevent sweat from evaporating, while the billowing robes trap sweat and recirculate it as cooler air. Guys in pants and shirts have to drink water constantly.

9/04 – smiles: learning the difference between crafty & honest

(aswan's felucca hustlers, egypt)

It's traditional for the traveler with time on his hands to rent a flat sailboat called a *felucca* and float gently down the Nile for a few days. A friend (whom I'd met in Cairo) and I were looking for a third to join us. Fortunately, the guy we met was an excellent judge of character and looked Egyptian enough to secure us a good deal.

9/05 - tourist attack
(abu simbel temple, egypt)

The entire imposing, and very ancient Abu Simbel temple was picked up and moved out of the way of a dam project in the 1960s (a feat of engineering that rivals the temple's original construction). Now, it stands in the middle of the desert, a lonely testament to a lost world (except for two times a day when it's invaded by snapshot-hungry aliens).

9/06 - lazy day on the nile
(felucca from aswan → edfu, egypt)

The *felucca* ride was amazing. As we silently glided down the river eating falafel for breakfast, lunch, and dinner, my eyes feasted on the rusted colors of the desert beyond the splash of green of the riverbank. I had been warned not to jump into the Nile, as it might make me ill, but overcome by a desire to swim where pharaohs had, I dived in anyway. The warnings were correct; I got sick.

9/07 - beating the water
to scare the fish into
the nets (felucca from
aswan → edfu, egypt

This guy probably has a cell phone now. . . .

9/08 - the wedding party & the forgotten bride
(Luxor, egypt)

One of the many advantages of exploring the small back alleys is that you might run across a neighborhood fete. You might even get invited to join in.

9/09 - girl shows a bicycle
shop & demands a tip
(luxor, egypt)

Even on the cheap, the difference between what I had and those around me
didn't have was stark. Children were the first line of savvy self-appointed
tour guides, trained to search out visitors and steer them in the direction of
their families' businesses while picking up a few coins. It can't be a pleasant
way to spend your childhood, but these kids did their jobs with impressive
professionalism. One boy caught me in a white lie when I claimed to be from
Holland. My American-accented Dutch didn't pass muster to his well-
trained ears.

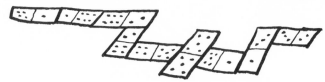

9/10 - my personal domino
advisers
(luxor, egypt)

Dominoes was second only to soccer as an Egyptian national passion. I
quickly picked up the habit of spending my afternoons playing at a café. I
loved it, even if my technique was off.

9/11 - one way to settle
a dispute (luxor, egypt)

What shocked me more was how the locals seemed to take this in stride.

9/12- face of a tourist trying to ride a donkey up a mountain with dignity
(valley of the Kings, egypt)

Sure, it seems romantic: approach the magical **Valley of the Kings** the old-fashioned way. But, halfway up the hill, cars were waiting for those who'd changed their minds. As for me, I pedaled around the temples on a rented bike, commuting from elaborate grave site to elaborate grave site with ease.

9/13 - the "hello" brigade
(asyot, egypt)

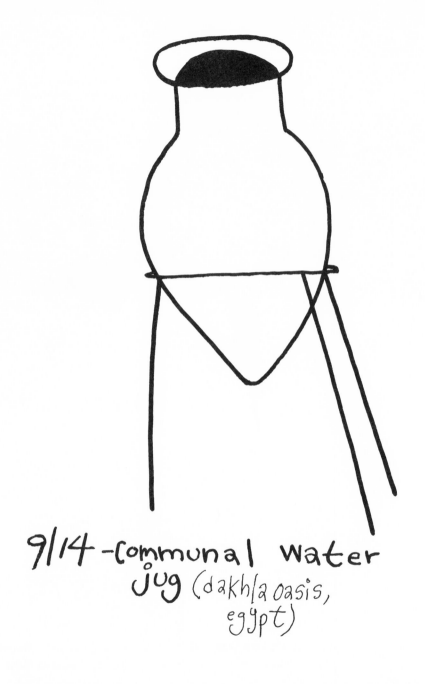

9/14 - communal water jug (dakhla oasis, egypt)

How beautiful. This simple, yet sturdy jug is the result of mere thousands of years of tinkering.

9/15 — the locals call him "mr. socks" (farafra oasis, egypt)

Remote by any standard, Farafra was a tiny oasis town accessible twice weekly by a tar road poured across the desert. The bus occasionally deposited some supplies or a backpacker or two. The village comprised a couple of hundred folks (all related in some way or other) and was chock-full of nutty characters. Mr. Socks, for example, had a penchant for foisting thick, hot, wool socks on his desert neighbors, most of whom wore sandals.

9/16 - boy & his horsey
(farafra, egypt)

Thanks to a local guy who invited me to share some of his extended family meals, I was able to get a glimpse of the rhythm of everyday Egyptian village life. I would spend my days with the camels, driving out to the desert, or checking out the village. (Large garish murals of buses, camels, and jet airplanes covered the walls of many of the dwellings, signs of how the home owners had transported themselves to Mecca on Hajj.)

9/17 - Badr, the artist.
certain that no one
understands him
(farafra oasis, egypt)

Enthusiastic and melancholy at the same time, Badr had spent years building a large compound largely out of sandy mud. The walls featured sand relief sculptures documenting important moments in his life, such as him building the compound documenting the important moments in his life . . . In addition to constructing a temple to himself and occasionally creating sand sculptures, Badr made plans for his dream project: a full-size scale model of the desert (scale 1 : 1).

9/18 - two egyptians
on the desert road
(bus farafra → cairo, egypt)

Throughout the Middle East and Indian subcontinent, people get from place A to place B by taking "Video Coaches," buses with poor suspension and blaring Bollywood tapes on shaky monitors. The vehicles' open windows serve as convenient travel-sickness disposal units.

9/19 - 4 letters from the american express office
(cairo, egypt)

Letters from friends became essential for my sanity. While traveling you might make a friend who you'd travel with for a few days or weeks, but I missed hearing from someone who already knew me.

9/20 – the six faces of
a bargain
(cairo, egypt)

Bargaining was the lifeblood of the merchant/tourist relationship. While it might be fun in the beginning, I quickly tired of it.

9/21 – guarding something really, very important (cairo, egypt)

Many "guards" had no ammunition in their rifles and everyone knew it. They were there to be employed, not guard.

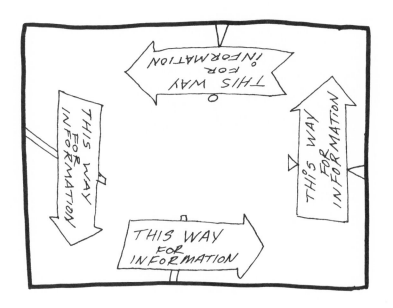

9/22- sending a parcel
(Cairo central post office, egypt)

A fantastical maze of halls, signs, and vast rooms with papers stacked to the ceilings awaiting the return of civil "servants" on "break," Cairo's fortresses of bureaucracy, like the post office, were astounding in their size and scale. Outside, a phalanx of photographers cluttered around the entrance, ready to produce photo-booth style head shots for various forms. Their cameras were simple wooden boxes, their shutters bottle caps that the cameramen took off of their lenses for a second or so. Each strip of pictures was developed on site in a series of chemicals under a heavy blanket. They made very cool pictures, though.

9/23 - boy watering tree in the street as if he planted it

(cairo, egypt)

Amid the smoke-belching madness of the car-, scooter-, truck-, donkey-, goat-, cat-, and people-filled streets were occasional moments of remarkable quietude.

9/24 - local party boss
makes a visit to his
people in the slums
(Karachi, Pakistan)

Like Cairo, Karachi bustled, but was much less free-spirited. Even to an outsider on his first day the cronyism and corruption were apparent.

9/25 - Shoes: 5 locals & 1 tourist
(Karachi, Pakistan)

Part of my Pakistani journey involved trying to avoid the only other Western traveler I encountered, a freaky guy who called himself "Squiddly Diddly" and giggled incessantly. Those are his sneakers (which, by the way, were bright pink). A few days later I came across sandals for the truly budget conscious: old truck tires cut into the shape of feet with strings nailed on as straps (proof that anything useful can find a second life).

9/26 - the locals act as
if i look like this
(karachi, Pakistan)

Unlike India, which had been inundated with backpackers since the '60s,
Pakistan had very little independent tourism.

9/27- carriage driver informs me that the only way into town is via carriage (moenjodaro, Pakistan)

More than five millennia old, Moenjodaro claims to be the first proper city in history. Its glory days passed quietly, so for most of recorded history it lay undisturbed and forgotten. Now that its red-brick foundations have been excavated from beneath the farmers' fields, the once-great city has become, understandably, a source of pride for Pakistanis. Unfortunately the modern pathways are constructed out of local brick nearly identical to that of the site's original ancient walls, which makes it difficult to discern what is five years old from what is 5,000.

9/28 - man who was given
free sample of eye-drops
(train: Larkana → Lahore,
Pakistan)

Trains are great places for traveling salesmen hawking all kinds of cures and ointments to improve one's looks or virility. The salesman who gave this guy a free sample would have to hope to make a sale from someone else.

By the way, it's considered pious for Muslim men to grow a beard similar to the Prophet's. For those who want to show their respect for Mohammed but hide their gray whiskers, the most common solution is to henna the beard, making it a bright, Day-Glo orange reminiscent of those '80s sweaters at The Limited.

9/29 - why can't you
ever find a rickshaw
when it monsoons?
(Lahore, Pakistan)

The water depth is no exaggeration and I couldn't take the subway. . . .

9/30 - agitated man
proudly displays his
gun license
(Lahore, Pakistan)

Not everyone was this disturbing by a long shot, but I found that many
would bring their stereotypes of a Yankee with them when they would meet
me; this guy figured I came from a gun-toting land and wanted to share
what we had in common.

EMBASSY of A. R. of EGYPT
TEL-AVIV
CONSULAR SECTION
TOURIST VISA No. 46202
VALIDITY THREE MONTHS

DATE OF ISSUE 27 -08- 1990

VALID FOR ONE ENTRY
PERIOD OF STAY ONE MONTH
FEES:
CONSUL GENERAL

PAKISTAN VISA
Number of Visa ___ 539/90
Type of Visa Entry/Transit/Tourist/Business
Date of Issue ___ 30 - 8 - 1990
Date of Expiry ___ 29 -11- 1990
No. of Entries: single / Dual / Multiple
Authorised Duration
of each stay ___ one month
Provided Passport remains valid
Purpose of Visit ___ Tourism

(MANZOOR UL HAQ)
Third Secretary
Embassy of Pakistan

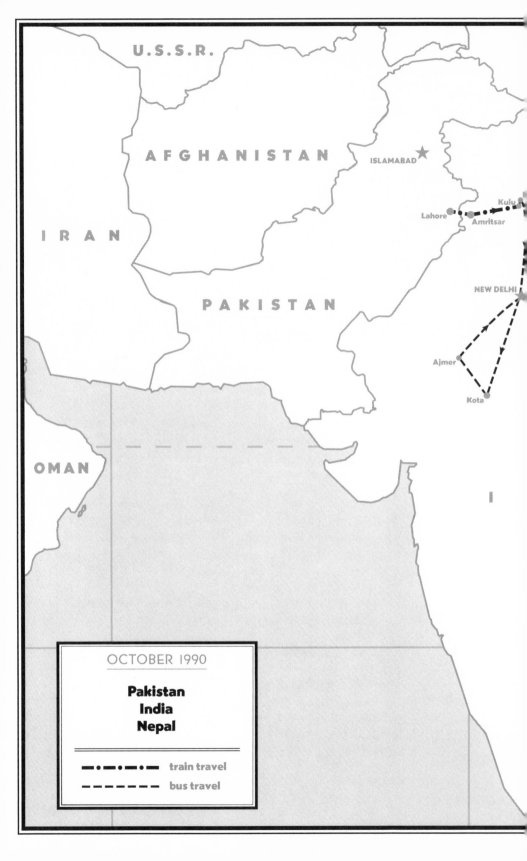

U.S.S.R.

AFGHANISTAN

ISLAMABAD ★

IRAN

PAKISTAN

Kulu

Lahore ● ● Amritsar

NEW DELHI

Ajmer

Kota

OMAN

OCTOBER 1990

**Pakistan
India
Nepal**

━ ·━ ·━ ·━ train travel

━ ━ ━ ━ ━ bus travel

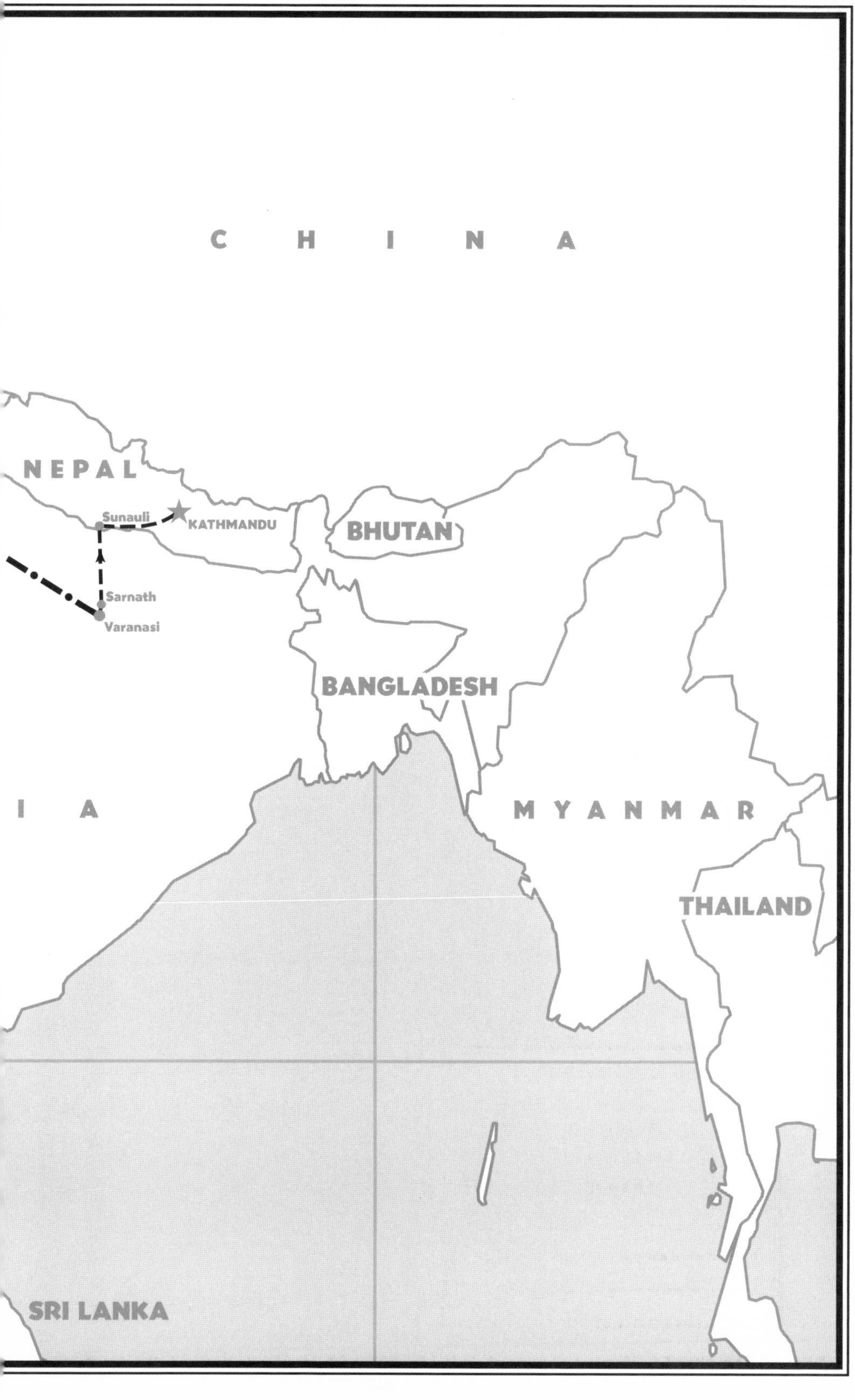

C H I N A
NEPAL
Sunauli
KATHMANDU
BHUTAN
Sarnath
Varanasi
BANGLADESH
I A
MYANMAR
THAILAND
SRI LANKA

10/01 - the sound that accompanies this is terrifying (Lahore, Pakistan)

The red-stained spit is a product of chewing betel, an indescribable concoction wrapped in a leaf and left to simmer in one's mouth. Some of the guys on the square thought they'd have a laugh and rolled me up a good big ol' betel. Its flavor possesses potency of a different magnitude than chewing tobacco. The taste sensation was prickly yet delicious for the first nanosecond or so; then I doubled over hacking and coughing. The guys had a ball watching me convulse, but they were good at heart and as a consolation prize they offered me a snack of goat's testicles (popular and supposedly good for one's potency).

10/02 - waiting in line
at passport control
(Lahore, Pakistan)

After the sudden shock of partition half a century ago, India and Pakistan have been in a constant state of hot and cold war. Consequently, the borders are difficult to pass. By crossing as a Westerner, I accomplished in one day what many Pakistanis and Indians couldn't despite years of paperwork and bribes.

1º/03 - sikh dresses son after dip in holy water
(golden temple, amritsar, india)

That Amritsar and the Sikh's Golden Temple can exist on the same land is amazing. The madness of livestock dodging buses, Vespas, and carriages along crowded, dusty roads in town instantly disappeared upon entering the temple—an iridescent central building that appeared to float idly in a giant reflecting pool surrounded by an ornate courtyard. All of the architectural beauty was enhanced by the fact that the temple was no showpiece. The joint was jumping: parents and children bathed in the pool, musicians played, and penitents prayed, all benignly ignoring the wandering tourists.

10/04- boy carries livestock's lunch (kulu, india)

Nestled at the start of the Himalayas, the Kulu Valley's charming woods and cooler temperatures helped it become a kind of Hamptons for India's upper crust while also attracting Tibetan refugees (Daramsala is nearby) and global hippies. Amidst all of this weirdness, a local, traditional world has managed to exist.

10/05 - fire & full moon
(old manali, india)

Devoid of city lights, the moon became my nightly guide, until it waned
(see 10/11)

10/06- Progress (manali, india)

10/07- mother & child
& chickens
(old manali, india)

Maybe they were on their way to play "Space Invaders."

10/08 - johnny: celebrity dope fiend, petty thief, & cook (beas cafe, old manali, india)

The café's expat scofflaws and dodgy traveling merchants had nothing on Johnny. He thrived in that gap between local and Western, crazy and sane, stoned and more stoned.

10/09- indian's opinion of my nationality expressed (old manali, india)

Part of being an American on the road is taking heat for American policy abroad, which is largely unpopular. A common pastime of clever Yankees, who think they can dodge difficult conversations about their nation, is to sew a Canadian flag on their backpacks, which only serves to hurt Canada's image abroad.

While I'm usually happy to try to discuss anything with anyone (at least until he picks up a flaming piece of firewood), the irony remains that many anti-America diatribes were delivered to me by people whose family members had (like my parents) emigrated to the States in search of a better life.

10/10 - i didn't make it
(vashisht, india)

Take-home message: shortcuts are not always shorter.

10/11 - night stroll
(old manali, india)

The darkness of the woods is unlike any I'd experienced. City slickers who spend their evenings in a café lodged in the middle of the woods are doomed to spend hours stumbling back to their electricity-free cabins.

10/12 – old man does his own thing & the freaks do theirs (ish café, old manali india)

The café scene was filled with dudes who arrived in the '70s and had forgotten to leave. Amid coughing chants of "boom-shanka," these mellow hippies chatted, drank tea, and occasionally made a dash for it (if the immigration police were in the hills). The cafés also invited an eclectic mix of locals who dug the scene and liked to dance.

10/13 – mourners bring their own wood to the funeral (old manali, india)

I'd see more funeral pyres in Varanasi (see 10/28), and was fascinated. Watching your dead relatives burn is profoundly weird (at least to me), but I guess it makes more sense than taking up ground to bury them.

10/14 - water pipe
made into toy
(old manali, india)

Okay, okay. I was spending too much time just hanging out in Manali. I was tired and wanted a break. I'll get going soon.

10/15 - bubba with balloons
(manali, india)

Fine. I'll go tomorrow. I promise.

10/16 - taxi driver's dilemma (New delhi, india)

The fear of being ripped off can be debilitating. Now I've learned to just get over it, but as a backpacker who counted every penny, I spent a lot of energy trying to avoid the "Gringo Tax."

10/17 - man blessing his cigarette stand before opening (new delhi, india)

What makes this so cool is how a guy could create a quiet moment amongst the madness and noise of downtown Delhi.

10/18 - Lethargy under
the big tent
(New delhi, india)

Years later this yawn of a circus inspired a comic strip I drew entitled "Freak Show of the Less-Than-Bizarre" featuring such attractions as the Bearded Man and the Slightly Paunchy Woman.

10/19- fruit seller (New delhi, india)

You'll buy a banana if you know what's good for you.

10/20 — one of these people is a pickpocket

(New delhi railway station, india)

I felt it happen, but wasn't quick enough to thwart the theft. Frustrated and embarrassed, I resolved never to be pickpocketed at a train station again. Sure enough, on the next attempt on my wallet (see 3/05), I saved my cash, but got bitten for my vigilance.

10/21- sunday drive
(New delhi, india)

Locally produced Vespas were the Indian equivalent to a Honda Civic in the States. I even saw larger families careening around the city, sometimes carrying gigantic Indian produced Victrolas on their heads.

10/22 - cow reflects on the indignities of being painted with orange spots & blue horns just for being holy (Kota, india)

Holy to the Hindu, India's cows have got it much better than their American cousins. Instead of worrying about the day they'll become burgers, Indian cattle stroll around unmolested and block traffic for hours without much complaint from the humans. I once sat in a restaurant and watched as a cow climbed the stairs and began eating the food off another patron's plate (holy cow!). The trade-off to the good life for cattle is having to get painted in silly designs and the occasional local Muslim giving you a swift kick when the Hindus aren't looking.

10/23- insect party
(my bed, ajmer, india)

I'm fairly certain that I spent that evening engaged in fascinating conversation with a local imam during a gaudy nighttime festival at the local mosque, but the biting bedbugs were so persistent, they won out for the day's cartoon.

10/24 - Kids impose a blockade To support a strike
(ajmer, india)

All was not well in India that fall. High-caste Hindu students set themselves on fire to protest the opening up of universities to other castes; Muslims and Hindus were battling over a plot of land used both as a temple and mosque; and hundreds of other turf wars that I couldn't comprehend raged throughout the north of the country. As I got on a local bus to Delhi, a mob instantly materialized and accosted our vehicle. Some deal must have been made, because after the driver yelled a few words, the mob parted briefly and let us out before attacking the other buses. This driver had seen it all before; tired of replacing windows broken by rock-tossing gangs, he'd taken all the windows out. The nighttime ride was breezy and cold, but at least we arrived in Delhi safely.

10/2⁵ – one of the rich, western indian teens (wimpy's burger, New delhi, india)

I returned to Delhi on business in 2001, and this scene was more the norm than the exception it had been in 1990.

10/26 - making dung patties
for future construction
(train: delhi → varanasi, india)

This, however, was still the norm in 2001 as well.

10/27 – lawn mowing
(sarnath, india)

And this.

10/28 - just another day
of public cremation
(burning ghat, Varanasi, india)

Varanasi is THE place to be cremated, and many pious elderly Hindus move
here so that they can be cremated on the banks of the holy Ganges river
when they die. The popularity of the site leads to a good deal of beautiful
hoopla, and some rather jaded priests.

10/29 - protesters looking for your support & more booze (bus from varanasi → sunauli, nepal)

Unrest was building around the country, with groups of radicalized Hindus (the orange team) and infuriated Muslims (the green team) staging large protests and small riots all over the place. Again, I managed to get out before real trouble started, on one of the last buses to Nepal. I discovered later that some friends who tried to leave the following morning found themselves stuck in their hostel as a general strike and mayhem shut down the town. They were forced to subsist on banana pancakes for two weeks.

10/30- little lady learns lugging (Sunauli → Kathmandu, nepal)

The steep, winding road to Kathmandu was in a state of constant disrepair as it snaked up the Himalayas; sections could be washed out by a flash flood or rendered impassible by rockfall in an instant. Consequently, it was wise to ride on the roof of the erratically driven buses, just in case the whole kit and caboodle plunged down a gorge. The uncertainty of the roadwork made wheels impractical for the majority of Nepalese, so alternate methods of lugging were required.

freak st

one block over

10/31- Kathmandu, nepal

Kathmandu was filled with varied mini-neighborhoods. The epicenter for the shaggy backpacker was Freak Street, where the mellowest cafés and pie shops abounded. The hipsters seldom left the few blocks, even to go to the more gung-ho trekker areas, much less the locals' alleys.

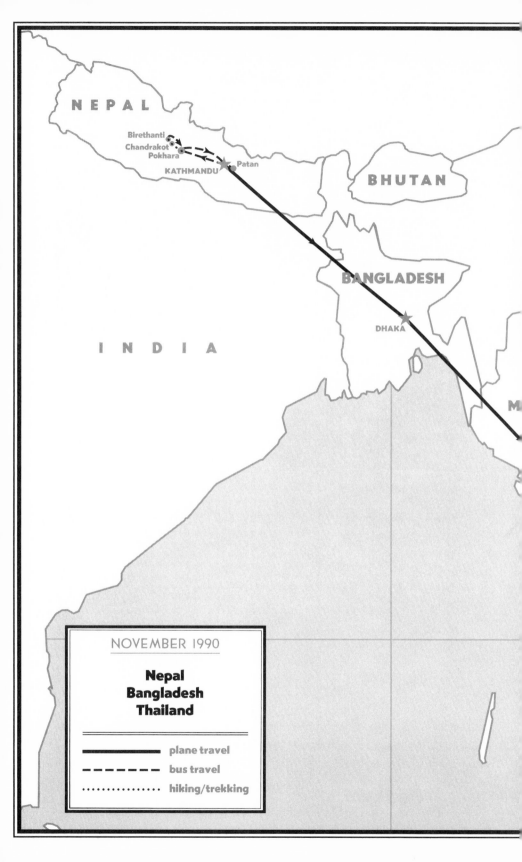

NEPAL

Birethanti
Chandrakot
Pokhara
KATHMANDU
Patan

BHUTAN

BANGLADESH

DHAKA

INDIA

M

NOVEMBER 1990

**Nepal
Bangladesh
Thailand**

———— plane travel

– – – – bus travel

·············· hiking/trekking

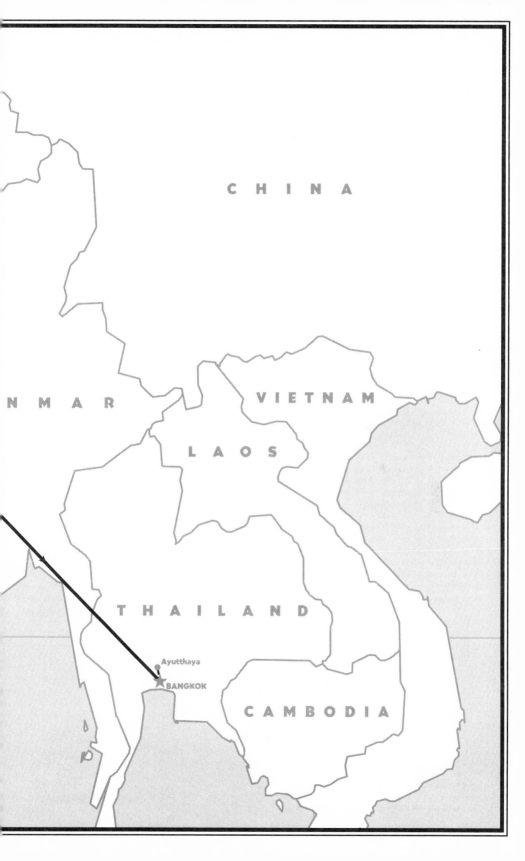

11/01 - "Well, i never!"
"oh, i know, i know!"
(kathmandu, nepal)

The gorgeous, intricately carved walls couldn't speak of all they had seen, but their inhabitants sure could.

11/oz–monkey's opinion of tourists (patan, nepal)

Street monkeys abounded in both Nepal and northern India. While most travelers' first impulse was to be charmed by monkeys ("Oh, they look like little people!"), they quickly discovered that the beasts were one step ahead of them. I met several folks who suddenly had their glasses or watches snatched by monkeys who wouldn't return them without a "liberation tax" of several bananas ("Oh, they *act* like people, too.").

11/03- pies (Kathmandu, nepal)

Although one's sense of judgment is usually impaired while visiting Freak Street, I swear that the cafés had the world's best apple pies ever.

11/04 - variations on a theme: cow horns
(bus Kathmandu → Pokhara, nepal)

Nothing like symmetrical horns to make one feel superior.

11/05 - body parts disagree on merits of a pony trek (pokhara, nepal)

In the battle of brain v. butt, the butt always wins.

11/06-different levels of zeal at the "folk dances of nepal" show (pokhara, nepal)

For most of the local performers, it was a living; but this guy was thinking, "Next stop: Broadway, baby!"

11/07 - tourist goes "nepal"
(Pokhara, nepal)

Many would land in Kathmandu from Europe and immediately dump their jeans to buy a whole "local" outfit (Tibet is in Nepal, right?). Yet, *somehow* the locals managed to figure out they were really tourists. . . .

11/08- boy practices herding by hurling rocks at passing cows
(Pokhara, nepal)

I'm not sayin', I'm just sayin', but this guy had a wicked slider.

11/09—the indignities of lugging hundreds of pounds of coke bottles wane in comparison to the mule's groovy hats
(trekking: Pokhara → chandrakot, nepal)

Trekking culture is the crunchy version of competitive high-school football. You seldom met a trekker without hearing how high, how far, and how dangerously they'd managed to trek. I felt like an unpopular fourth grader again, as robust trekkers dissed me for refusing to go where no Gurkha had gone before. Naively, I figured that if local mountain people thought somewhere was too dangerous, they knew what they were talking about. Weakness! I was prepared to hear hours of machismo on the first day's trek uphill. Fortunately, the "true" trekkers were so busy Velcro-ing and re-Velcro-ing their backpacks, I had a chance to enjoy the pack mule's cool costume.

11/10 - today i walked so hard, my leg fell off
(trekking: chandrakot → birethanti, nepal)

Remember that hernia I got in Turkey (8/08)? Suddenly, I did.

But whatever you've trekked up, you need to trek down. The last chance for me to become a "true" trekker lost, I could focus on my debilitating pain.

$1^1/1^2$ – new York shrink
explains italian's desire
to holiday in nepal as
escaping her mother
(pokhara, nepal)

You cannot escape New York.

11/13 - using cuteness to sell bananas (bus: Pokhara → Kathmandu, nepal)

Having failed at trekking and desperate for a few nights in the same bed, I chose to take some time and just hang in Kathmandu, a cool town filled with exuberant Hindu and Buddhist art and architecture. Luckily, I ran into a bunch of pals I'd made back in Egypt and India. So, I got to spend some days walking around and visiting friends; it was almost like I lived there.

11/14 - Street seller tries to make one last sale before dusk (Kathmandu, Nepal)

This was the only souvenir I purchased during my trip. Today it hangs above my desk.

11/15-buddhist on bike
(kathmandu, nepal)

Nestled in the steep Himalayas, Kathmandu's got some great slopes for gliding on your bike.

11/16 - Sadu who blesses for profit (Kathmandu, nepal)

India and Nepal were awash in groups of wandering itinerant Sadus (holy men) of varying degrees of holiness. Some seemed to be in it for the quick buck, others minded their own business. One Sadu surprised a straightlaced couple I knew when he popped out of the blue, said, "You need this," and gave them big bag of grass before disappearing into the crowd.

11/17 – deity nook (patan, nepal)

An elephant-headed Ganesh can help businesses prosper, so why not put him in the alcove of a market street?

$1^1/1^8$-big money to be won at marbles (Kathmandu, Nepal)

You can bet on anything.

11/19 - Laundry day
(kathmandu, nepal)

Even if the trekkers didn't think I was the real deal, after almost six months on the road I was granted dubious respect and a wide berth by those who'd only been on the road for a month or so. Perhaps it was my telltale odor, but I was considered a "traveler" now (an honor to be sure, but I yearned for some clean underwear instead).

11/20 - rooftops
(Kathmandu, nepal)

Kathmandu's central square (where the Hindu "living goddess" resides) is beautiful and bustling, particularly at sunset. After a few days, I'd made friends with the hordes of kids hawking Tiger Balm to the tourists. We hung out, and I doodled as they dashed back and forth among the occasional busloads of German tourists.

11/21 - butterfly says
hello (kathmandu, nepal)

$1^1/22$ - Frenchman in Room 401 who lost his puppy
(kathmandu, nepal)

The buck-a-night hostel where I'd rented a room rapidly took on a sitcom-esque life of its own. This guy was the Kramer who stumbled into everyone's room at some point (usually an inconvenient point at that) to ask after his missing puppy. After a week or so, I think he found it only to discover that he couldn't take it back to France with him.

11/23 - dealer who is so
stoned his stuff must
be good (freak st., kathmandu,
nepal)

Some dudes are best avoided.

1¹/24 - the victor & the victim (kathmandu, nepal)

The temptation to order Western style food (particularly meat) in a non-Western environment has its price. I paid in full.

11/25 - the paperwork to send a parcel outweighs the parcel itself (Kathmandu, Nepal)

Most Asian central post offices included phone banks where you could (after a suitably long wait) place a collect call abroad. I phoned home perhaps once a month for five minutes or so. It was profoundly weird to suddenly chat with family, then hang up and instantly be back halfway across the world again, alone.

11/26 – 11 hours of islamic
hits just isn't enough
for jambox owner
(dhaka airport, bangladesh)

My plan to visit Bangladesh (usually not a place high on the list of holiday destinations) was thwarted by an uprising in Dhaka just as my flight landed. The authorities quickly announced that we wouldn't be allowed out of the airport for at least a few days. A cursory look outside, where men were dashing to and fro with guns and machetes, reinforced the wisdom of remaining in the airport lobby.

11/27 - 19 hours of it,
however is more than
enough for me (dhaka airport,
bangladesh)

The unrest continued with no end in sight. Luckily, I managed to get a flight to Thailand (mostly to escape that infernal boom box).

11/28– meat market &
kentucky fried chicken
(Bangkok, thailand)

The backpackers' section of Bangkok shares real estate with the fleshpot clubs and fast-food joints, creating one of the most depressing areas I've ever visited.

1¹/29 – buddha in the back
(bangkok, thailand)

Some nations' religious affiliations are inescapable (Italy's Roman Catholicism, for example). For Thailand it was Buddhism. Even in the most "modern" sections of Bangkok, icons and monks' saffron-colored cloaks abounded (partially because it's traditional for boys to spend a few of their preteen years as monks).

11/30 - buddhas in the grass
(wat Phra mahathat, ayutthaya, thailand)

Thailand's fantastic ruins (huge ancient temple complexes filled with decaying statuary) were fun to tramp through. The ruins were gloriously large and charmingly disorganized. It wasn't hard to get lost among the giant trees supporting the crumbling walls of the temples while sidestepping all the huge merrily decapitated Buddhas. I also ran into a lady from the Upper East Side of Manhattan who wanted to set me up with her daughter when I finished my travels.

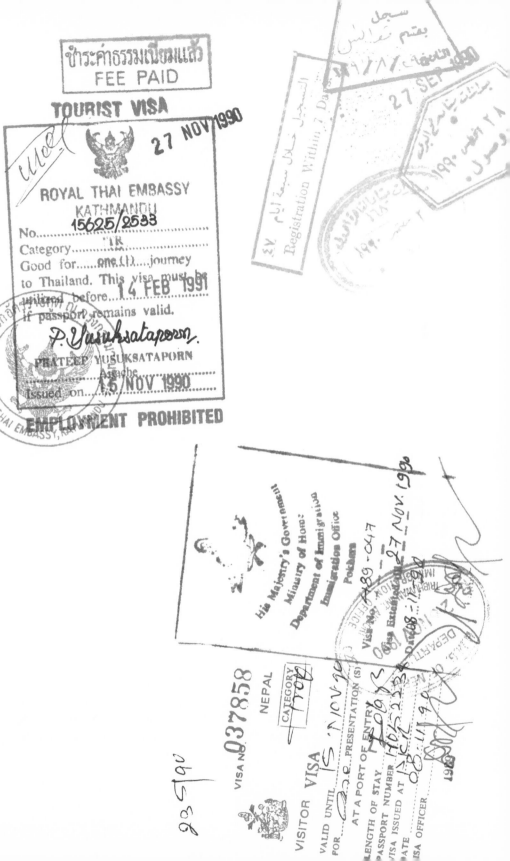

ชำระค่าธรรมเนียมแล้ว
FEE PAID

TOURIST VISA

27 NOV 1990

ROYAL THAI EMBASSY
KATHMANDU
No. 15625/2533
Category TR
Good for one (1) journey
to Thailand. This visa must be
utilized before 14 FEB 1991
if passport remains valid.

P. Yusuksataporn.
PRATEEP YUSUKSATAPORN
Attache
Issued on 15 NOV 1990

EMPLOYMENT PROHIBITED

Registration Within 7 Days

27 SEP 1990

NEPAL

VISA No. 037858

CATEGORY

VISITOR VISA

His Majesty's Government
Ministry of Home
Department of Immigration
Immigration Office
Pokhara

27 NOV 1990

VALID UNTIL 15 NOV 20..

FOR 22.0. PRESENTATION (S)

AT A PORT OF ENTRY

LENGTH OF STAY

PASSPORT NUMBER

VISA ISSUED AT

DATE

VISA OFFICER

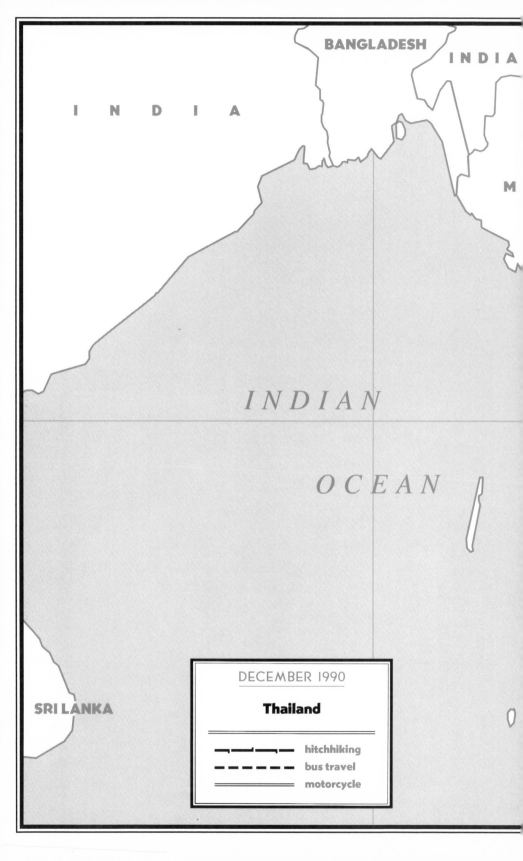

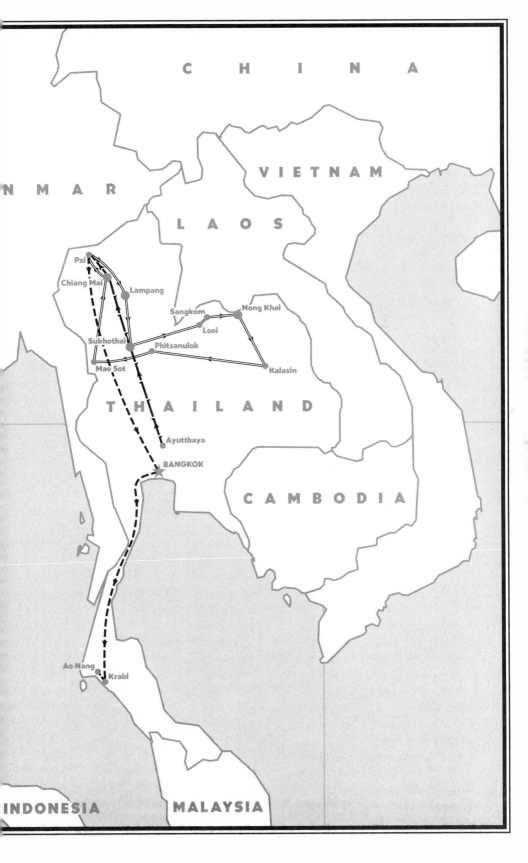

12/01 - having a drink with the guys (ayutthaya, thailand)

The tiger tattoos are intended to make one invulnerable to attack, but they can't protect you from a swollen nose when you drunkenly trip and fall.

12/02 - having forgotten incense, man hopes buddha will accept a cigarette
(sukhothai, thailand)

A stop at the local temple was a must in Thailand, even if you came unprepared.

12/03 - truck-driving father & son have lunch
(hitching: sukhothai → chiang mai, thailand)

Thailand is the start of what I call "The Great Hitcher's Crescent" that descends from the northern Thai hill country through Malaysia, ending abruptly at Singapore (everything fun ends abruptly at Singapore). The advantages of hitchhiking are many: you get to meet a great number of locals who aren't involved in the tourist trade, you usually end up sharing a meal with your new friends, and it's free. The downside in most countries is the long wait, but in the "Hitcher's Crescent" that was seldom an issue.

12/04— Wicker ball version
of no-hands Volleyball
(chiang mai, thailand)

Fun to watch, impossible to get over the net. Even more impressive, some of the kids could play this game with devastating skill even though they were wearing clunky monk's robes.

12/05 - top brass salute
King's birthday with candles
(chiang mai, thailand)

Buddhism, power, and celebrity combined in Thai's devotion to their king, by all accounts a real good guy who remains above politics, unless those in power are really messing things up. Considering that Thailand has managed to escape its neighbors' propensity for war and tyranny, digging the king makes sense.

12/06 - Street vendor makin'
roti, sellin' roti, & crackin'
jokes just as fast as he
can (Pai, Thailand)

Every town in Thailand had a large open-air central market where you could
get just about anything, including a great meal cooked up quick. In the
evening, the village's population would converge on the markets to browse
for socks, audiotapes of pop stars, or live chickens, before ordering up some
Pad Thai. In Pai, everyone seemed to order this guy's delicious rotis (sweet,
yummy crepe-like thingies) for dessert, partially because he was so much
fun to watch.

12/07 - picnickers boil their eggs in the hot springs
(Pai, thailand)

Hot springs abound throughout Thailand, Malaysia, and Indonesia. Unlike in the litigious States, there are no protective barriers between visitors and the boiling, sulfur-spewing natural wonder. So, if you don't mind getting accidentally burned, you can use the springs as you wish.

12/08 – mopeding in the mountains (pai →
Lampang, thailand)

I decided to rent a small motorcycle for a few weeks and buzz around Thailand, a choice I rationalized by saying it was the only way to see parts of the country not easily accessible by bus. The truth was it was cool to scoot around the gorgeous, empty, winding mountain roads.

12/09- while ordering lunch i make a mental note to learn the thai word for "chicken"
(moped: lampang → sukhothai, thailand)

And what was more embarrassing for me was discovering that the Thai language ends common phrases with a suffix denoting the speaker's sex. A literal translation of what I said: "Hello (I'm a woman). May I have some BAAAWK! BAAAWK! BAAAWK! with rice, please (I'm a woman)." Good on 'em for not laughing louder.

12/10 - fresh bread on the street (Loie, thailand)

The towns got smaller and the lifestyles more traditional. Great-tasting bread, by the way.

12/11- Fishing (moped: loie → sangkom, thailand)

Beautiful waterfalls and people fishing on the Mekong river abounded. And, I managed to barter a night's rest and hot sauna for drawing up a flyer promoting the local hostel.

12/12 - boy struggles up the
mekong river (sangkom, thailand)

The eternal rhythms of village life, now with a Lakers shirt!

12/13 – some how, this sign does little to reassure me (moped: Sangkom → Nangkhai thailand)

Being so close to the Laos border, there were many military bases in the area. The signs were a friendly reminder for drunken soldiers.

12/14 - officer demands to see my driver's license, but since he can't read english, he lets me go (Kalasin, thailand)

It's not so much that I shouldn't have been motorbiking around the area, it was just too unusual for the cop not to do something.

12/15 – this young man was certain i was speaking fluent thai (moped: Kalasin ⟶ phitsanulok, thailand)

Odd that this weird scene would make my sketch, because it was around here that I encountered a large garden filled with wild, monstrous cement statues built by a local eccentric. The fantastical creatures were all based on visionary dreams which compelled him to bring them to life in commercial cement. The visions, which had started small as odd life-size monkey gods or snakes, grew over the years until they demanded three- or four-story tall snake-god monsters.

12/16 - shaking sticks to say "amen" to buddha*
(phitsanulok, thailand)

* KNOWN AS "SAEM SAE"

And it made a beautiful sound.

12/17 - children from local Karen
hill tribe come a-carolin'
(mae sod, thailand)

The Karen are locked in a battle with the neighboring Burmese government for control of their homeland. While some children stayed in Myanmar and became mystic, cigar chomping, hard-living guerilla leaders, others lived as refugees in Thailand.

12/18 - buy this caged bird
so you can do the good
deed of releasing it
(buddhist temples, moped: mae sod →
chiang mai , thailand)

A reminder that even kindness can be turned into an industry.

12/19 – old man reaches for a rock & the dogs scatter
(moped: chiang mai → pai, thailand)

A game this guy found endlessly amusing, and because I was waiting to get my motorbike fixed, I got to watch it for hours.

12/20- Karen hill tribe member
in local folk costume
(pai, thailand)

So, here I am in a rather inaccessible mountainous section of northern Thailand, but like anywhere else on the planet that year, illustrator Sue Rose's goofy Fido Dido was the coolest thing around. A year or so after my trip, I met Sue in New York while looking for illustration work. A nice lady, she had no idea of her doodle's global omnipresence.

12/21- after two hours on the bus, remembering i forgot my passport in pai (bus: pai → bangkok, —thailand)

One of the drags of long trips is having to carry your essentials (passport, credit card, cash) day in and day out. Slowly, that little pouch dangling around your neck starts to drive you mad. But, take it off and it exacts its revenge.

12/22 - this man's yoke is
little sugar cakes
(bangkok, thailand)

Southeast Asia was an odd melding of twentieth-century technology (cars, trucks, electric signs) and ancient (but effective) modes of transportation.

12/23 - the beach bus stops
by the village
(Krabi → Ao Nang beach, thailand)

It was shocking for me to come into contact with party-bound tourists out for a few weeks of fun and sun. After over half a year on the road, they felt more alien to me than the lady with the chicken.

12/24 - shopping for books
(KRabi, thailand)

Reading material becomes precious after a few months backpacking. Many hipster-traveler inns have small "trading libraries" where you can exchange your finished book for a new one. It's a great system, except for the caveat that you have to exchange for a thinner book. This policy took me from Iris Murdoch to *Benji* to Graham Greene to a Mod Squad novelization to Machiavelli's *The Prince*. There's nothing thinner than *The Prince*, so I had to look for something new at the fourth-hand beach bookstore.

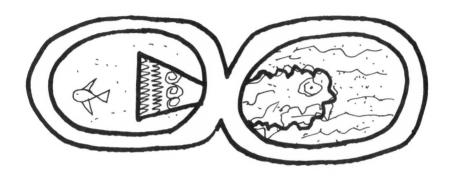

12/25 - my right goggle fills up with water
(Ao Nang beach, thailand)

For Christmas, I went snorkeling for the first time. It was lovely for the few seconds I wasn't being blinded by the water, scratching myself against the coral, or gagging on my water intake.

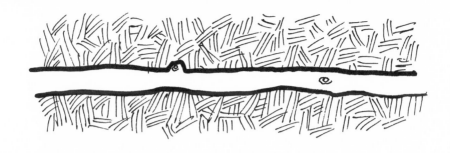

12/26 - lamp, whiskey, matches
(Ao Nang, thailand)

It was a beautiful, warm evening as I rested in my romantic little straw hut on stilts. Countless tourists were doing the same thing fifteen years later when the terrible tsunami struck. I cannot imagine it, yet it felt very close as I saw photographs of the devastation in 2004.

12/27 - major tourist attraction: old videos (cafés, ao Nang beach, thailand)

A Bond movie had been shot there years ago, and the glorious shot of a towering island in the midst of the blue water (which served as the villain's retreat) is what exposed many of the tourists to the beauty of coastal Thailand. The story goes that there were actually two giant islands, but the director thought the second one cluttered the shot, so had it destroyed.

12/28 - everyone loves the monkey, & he knows it
("Jungle huts", Ao Nang, Thailand)

Every hostel seemed to have its own monkey. I never much cottoned to the animals, partially because I found their consistent horniness distracting during meals.

12/29- beach fashion:
less is more
(Ao Nang beach, thailand)

Yikes.

12/30- learning to ride before you walk
(Ao Nang, Thailand)

The kids would scamper up giant palm trees for a few coconuts, then zip off
on their scooters. When I was that age, watching cartoons was about all the
excitement I ever got.

12/31 - daddy helps baby with sand castle & forgets about baby (Ao Nang beach, Thailand)

Three words you never want to hear in a row: German. Beach. Wear.

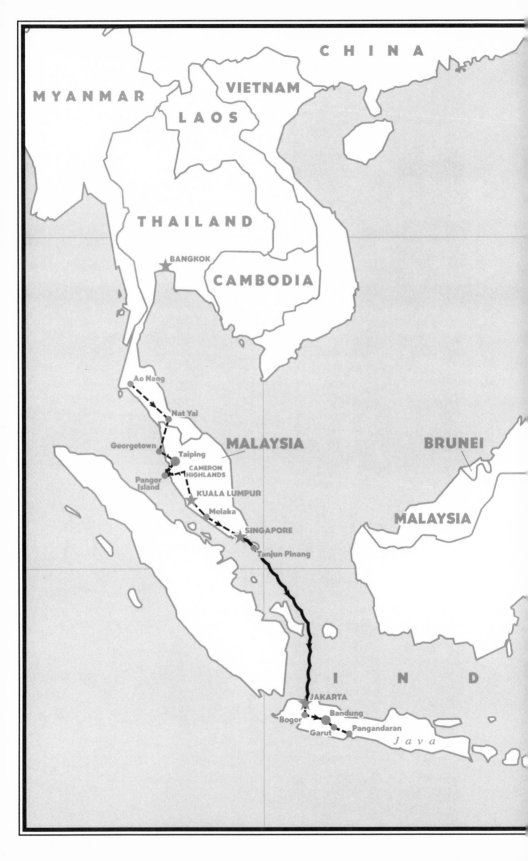

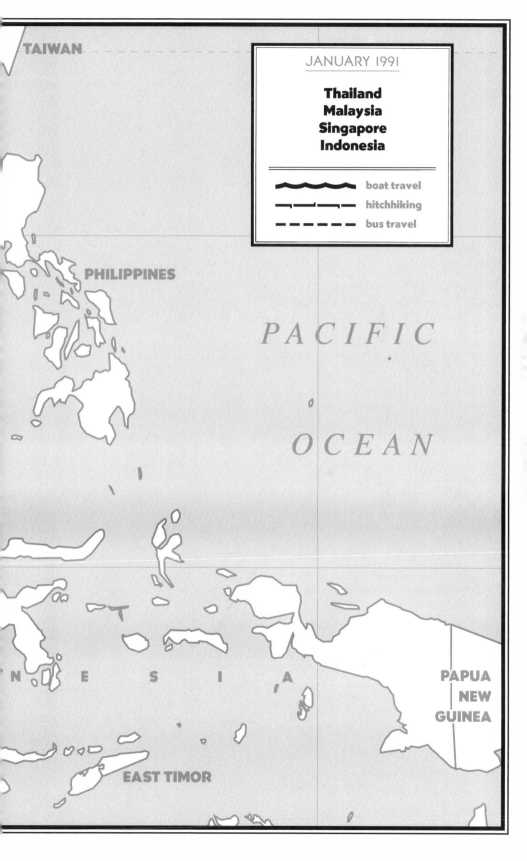

TAIWAN

PHILIPPINES

JANUARY 1991

Thailand
Malaysia
Singapore
Indonesia

〜〜〜〜 boat travel

—■—■— hitchhiking

— — — — bus travel

PACIFIC

OCEAN

N   E   S   I   A

EAST TIMOR

PAPUA
NEW
GUINEA

1/1/92 - morning: i make
Some resolutions as to how
i'll spend next new year's
eve (Ao Nang, thailand)

Enough lazy hedonism for me, it was time to get back on the road.

1/02 - seamstress working
under highway bridge
(hat yai, thailand)

I spent the majority of the year in the same pair of pants. As the need arrived, I'd have them patched with local cloth. In most countries clothing is not as disposable as it is in the States, so it usually just took a quick stroll to find an area filled with people with old foot-powered sewing machines. This time I got a nice patch on the butt.

1/03 - malaysian muslim
does his best to sport
a proper islamic beard
(georgetown, malaysia)

Georgetown (like much of Malaysia) was a fantastic, scrunched-up mix of native Malay, Indian, and Chinese culture with Arab ideas. Here a Muslim's devotion to beards wasn't always effective.

1/04 - burning holy money
so he can have money
to burn in the after-
life (georgetown, malaysia)

One of the deals with ancestor worship is the obligation to forward symbolic cash to your departed elders to make their afterlife more comfortable. This idea reaches its logical conclusion when you want to send something more personal than money (see 1/16).

1/05 - 40-year-old truck driver is doing so well he could afford a 2ⁿᵈ wife, if he wanted one (hitching: georgetown → taiping, malaysia)

Generous, witty, and exuberant about his lot in life, this gentleman insisted on filling me with fresh coconut milk as he pointed proudly to the roots of a tree that (when sliced correctly) resemble the Arabic calligraphy of the word "Allah."

1/06 - mommy points out the
funny funny monkey to baby
(taiping, malaysia)

This zoo was filled with the exact same breed of monkey that could be found wandering throughout the town's streets and public parks. In fact, gangs of the town's free monkeys would occasionally visit the zoo to tease their imprisoned cousins.

1/07 - modesty makes
maidens swim fully
dressed (pangkor island, malaysia)

In Egypt, women swam in full chadors, so I suppose this was a bit racy.

1/08 - gringo demonstrates the making of a "sandwich"
(pangkor island, malaysia)

After a while many backpackers have had enough of local food and yearn for childhood delicacies.

1/09- child plays with fish
daddy just caught
(pangkor island, malaysia)

More than a meal: they're toys!

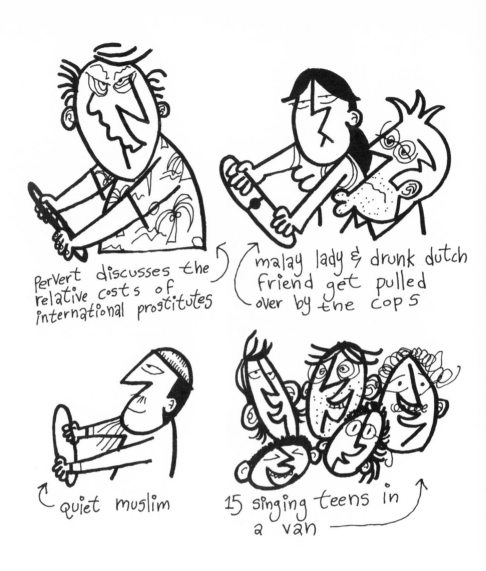

1/10- all in a days hitch
(pangkor isl. → cameron highlands, malaysia)

Even more than Thailand, Malaysia was a hitching paradise. I never had to wait more than a few minutes for a ride, although sometimes I wished I had.

1/11— and at the other end of the park the girls are giggling (cameron highlands,) malaysia

Some things are universal (even if the haircuts are not).

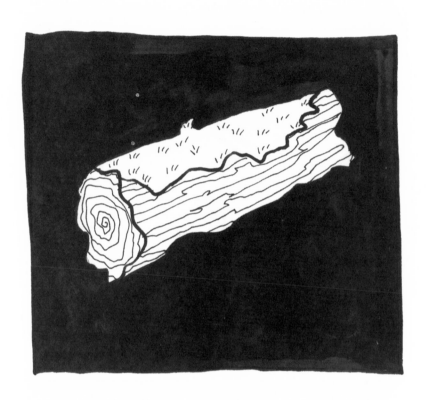

1/12- fungus-covered log
(cameron highlands, malaysia)

Filled with tea plantations and backpackers' cafés, the highlands had the added attraction of expansive forests where one could wander for hours.

1/13- salesman & his new, fantastic, scientifically formulated, magic rust remover (cameron highlands, malaysia)

The huckster traveling salesmen may have vanished from the American landscape, but East Asia was full of them. They always put on a great show.

1/14 - freelance sellers of bus tickets (Kuala Lumpur, malaysia)

Ugh. Either I was getting more tired of being badgered or these guys were getting more aggressive.

1/15 - begging to music
(Kuala Lumpur, Malaysia)

After visiting small villages, the scale of Kuala Lumpur was disorienting. It was like being back in Manhattan, only crazier, busier, and I didn't remember Kentucky Fried Chicken providing porcelain ashtrays with the Colonel's face in New York.

1/16 - cardboard goodies to burn for the after life
(malacca, malaysia)

Devoted Malay Chinese burn ceremonial money for their deceased ancestors to spend while in the afterlife (see 1/04). But for the descendant who really cares, fake, flammable appliances are available. My favorite: the VCR for ethereal spirits on the go. Note the brand, Hellevision!

1/17 - two birds in a cage, no sugar in my tea, & a war in the gulf (malacca, malaysia)

Fifteen years later, and it's still true.

1|18—options (singapore)

After easygoing Thailand and Malaysia, Singapore was one big "DO NOT" sign. This is a city-state where chewing gum was banned and many prosperous neighborhoods dispensed with sidewalks to discourage those without cars from visiting.

1/19- man suffers mall shock
(singapore)

But you could always buy something.

1/20 - Shoe-Shine boy
(tanjung pinang, sumatra, indonesia)

The boat to Java departs from Tanjung Pinang, so the town is filled with people just waiting around for their ship, the perfect place for a shoe-shine boy to ply his trade, even if you're wearing sandals.

1/21- Kids sit on stoop
(tanjung Pinang, sumatra, indonesia)

Boat, train, and bus schedules are more optimistic than realistic in most parts of the world. A friend I met in Egypt related an example from his trip to the Sudan. He bought a ticket (with assigned seating) on a bus to Aswan and waited five hours for it to arrive. When the bus opened its doors, my friend discovered a ticketed gentleman already in his seat. Confused as to how two people could have tickets for the same seat, he was informed, "Oh, you have a ticket for *today's* bus. This is *yesterday's* bus. *Today's* bus comes tomorrow." The point being, don't rush, because you can't do anything about it anyway. Better to spend the extra day hanging on the stoop like these kids until your ship arrives.

1/22 - Ship's cook serves rice with a shovel
(boat: tanjung pinang → jakarta, java, indonesia)

It was a long, bumpy journey with little to do; but the rice wasn't half bad. It was three-quarters bad.

1/23 - after 32 hours at sea, the captain announces the safety procedures
(boat: tangung pinang → jakarta, java indonesia)

1/24 - dredging the muck from the sewers (Jakarta, Java, indonesia)

A former Dutch colony, Indonesia at the time was ruled with a corrupt iron fist. I'm not sure what that has to do with dredging muck up from under the streets, but . . .

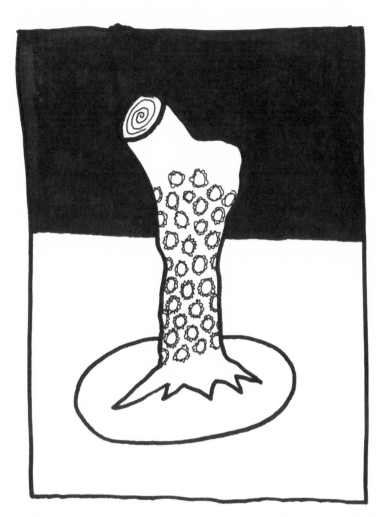

1|25 – tree stump decorated with bottle caps (Jakarta, Java, indonesia)

These bits of, well, I guess you'd call them folk art were everywhere. Strangely beautiful, they denoted a society that likes soda.

1/26 - card game in the middle of a packed train (Jakarta → bogor, java, indonesia)

The best adaptation to constantly being stuck in crowds is to ignore it.

1/27-high-rise apartment
(bandung, java, indonesia)

These traditional huts are every little boy's dream house.

1/28- bats still seem to be figuring out this Flying thing (garut, java, indonesia)

Which was not the case with the giant fruit bats at Pangandaran (see 1/31). Impressive flocks of them (each with a six-foot wingspan) would slowly, gracefully blacken the sky at dusk as they commuted to the nearby fruit plantations.

1/29- testing the water in the hot-spring bath
(garut, java, indonesia)

A volcanic island to begin with, Java is dotted with great hot springs. This simple resort had cobbled together an aqueduct of naturally scalding water running through every room. Just yank out the oversized cork on the side and you'd fill your eight-foot cube bath.

1/30- horse's raingear
(garut, java, indonesia)

Java features a wet season followed by a wetter season, hence the lush forests and silly hats.

1/31-communication (pangandaran, java, indonesia)

Ugh. Monkeys.

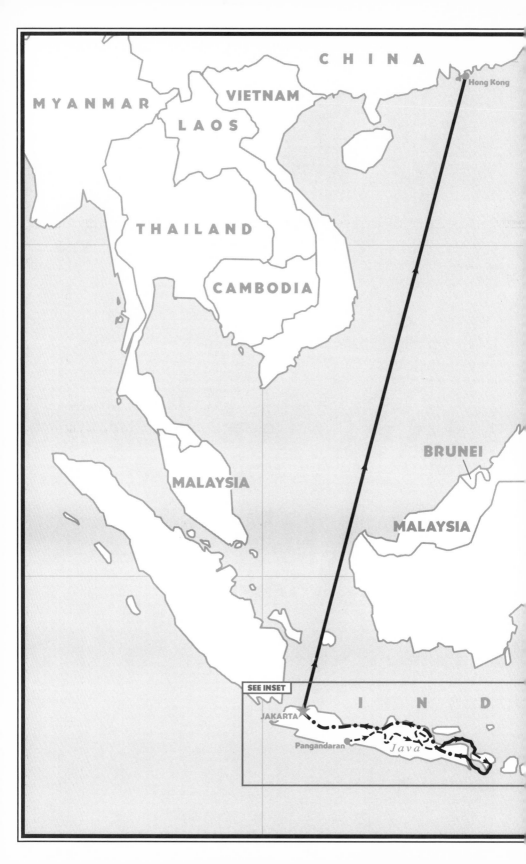

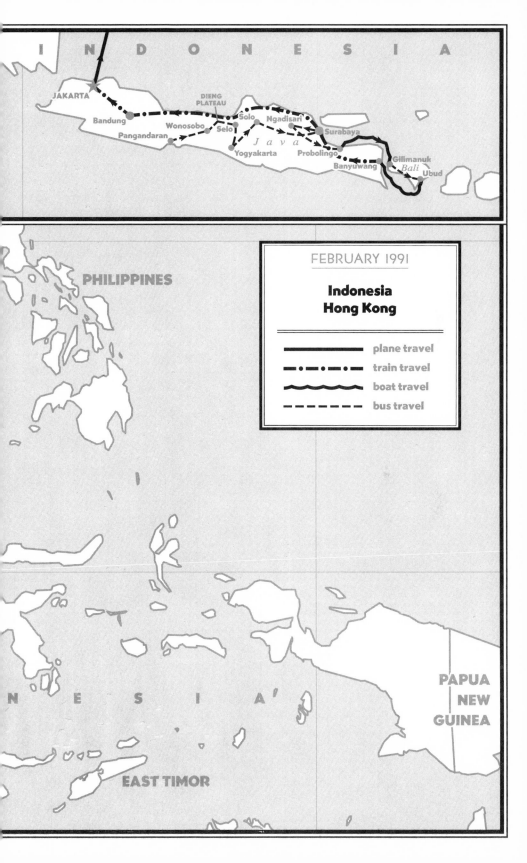

INDONESIA

JAKARTA

Bandung

Pangandaran

Wonosobo

DIENG
PLATEAU

Solo

Selo

Ngadisari

Surabaya

Yogyakarta

Probolinggo

Banyuwang

Gilimanuk

Ubud

Java

Bali

FEBRUARY 1991

**Indonesia
Hong Kong**

plane travel
train travel
boat travel
bus travel

PHILIPPINES

I N D O N E S I A

EAST TIMOR

PAPUA
NEW
GUINEA

2/1- bringin' home the bacon (pangandaran, java, indonesia)

Who needs supermarkets?

2/2 - When the price is two hundred (boat, bus: pangandaran → wonosobo, java, indonesia)

Bargaining, the bane of travel.

2/3- the old tobacco seller with his special mix of cloves (wonosobo, java, indonesia)

While his withered appearance and hacking cough weren't the best advertising for his product, this gentleman produced some delicious smokes.

2/4 - bubbling mud at the steaming craters
(dieng plateau, java, indonesia)

Stunning, spectacular, and smelly, the vast fields of steaming, acrid stuff could be explored at one's leisure. But watch out for the sections where you suddenly found yourself sinking into the hot, mushy earth.

2/5-making big rocks into
small rocks (bus: Wonosobo ⟶
selo, java, indonesia)

I still flash back on this whenever I drive on a gravel road.

2/6- mountain view
(selo, java, indonesia)

Hillside farms covered every inch of land possible (see also 2/17).

2/7-market day (selo, java, indonesia)

Everything and everyone in the hills had a different, dizzying texture.

2/8 - pleasant little midnight stroll (mt. merapi, Selo, java, indonesia)

The rationale for visiting the village of Selo was as a staging post to the once-in-a-lifetime experience of viewing the sunrise from atop volcanic Mount Merapi. Unfortunately, the night a friend and I attempted to reach the summit coincided with a massive storm that damaged several homes. I can only hope that the sunrise I witnessed while sliding down the muddy, tree-strewn mountain will be a once-in-a-lifetime experience.

2/9 - sidewalk parking attendants (Yogyakarta, java, indonesia)

The cultural capital of Java, Yogyakarta was a wild sea of swerving traffic; the perfect opportunity for self-appointed parking managers.

2/10–bad day for the hand-crafted tribal blow-dart gun salesman
(Yogyakarta, java, indonesia)

Seriously, who's gonna squeeze a four-foot-long blow-dart gun in their carry-on?

2/11 - the gecko hunters
(Yogyakarta, Java, indonesia)

It's unfortunate that the kids got such a kick out of this. Geckos eat mosquitoes; the more geckos in your hotel room, the better.

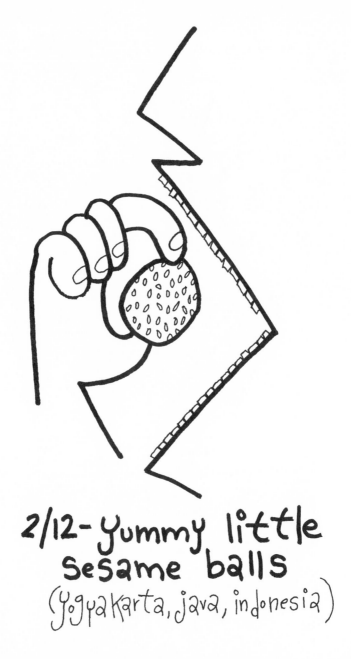

2/12 - yummy little sesame balls
(Yogyakarta, java, indonesia)

As a birthday present to myself, I'd spent 15 bucks the previous night for a room in a vintage '70s motel with air-conditioning and a mildewed swimming pool; a luxurious step up from my normal "dormitory style" lodging. The rest of the day was spent indulging in my favorite Indonesian treat.

2/13-how i handle rick-shaw drivers hassling me

(bus: yogyakarta → solo, java, indonesia)

Some of these fellows would follow me for blocks before giving up on me. They had a living to make, but a surly backpacker with huge sideburns and a snarl would not seem to be worth the bother.

2|14-minstrel & his
portable speaker
system (solo, java, indonesia)

The American exchange: we get your oil, we'll give you rock 'n'roll.

2/15 - villagers come 'round to watch bus stuck in the mud (bus: Solo → surabaja, java, indonesia)

A traveler learns never to be in a hurry on Indonesia's rainy, muddy roads. It's "everybody off the bus" and meet the locals.

2/16 - coffee out of the saucer (Ngadisari, java, indonesia)

I have no idea how normal this is, or if this guy was just a local character, but, man, that sound was something fearsome.

2/17-cabbage farmer
lives his life on the
edge (ngadisari, java, indonesia)

2/18 - scarecrow traffic cops (probolinggo, java, indonesia)

It's my understanding that this law-enforcement innovation has made it to the highways of America. Papier-mâché criminals around the world tremble.

2/19- the almost thief
(bus, ferry: probolinggo, java ⟶
gilimanuk, bali, indonesia)

2/20 - off to the temple for offerings (ubud, bali, indonesia)

I only spent a few days in Bali, and while I found it overly dependent on its tourist trade, the island and its people really were beautiful.

2/21- the friendly dogs of bali (ubud, bali, indonesia)

Its canine population, on the other hand . . .

2/22-little blessings
(every corner, ubud, indonesia)

The religiosity of the people was undeniable; almost every activity involved some sort of votive moment.

2/23- old lady & baby chicks
(ubud, bali, indonesia)

In some extended families, it was granny's job to watch the livestock.

2/24- child's first punk
(banyuwangi train station, java, indonesia)

"Travel! Meet the people of the world and scare them!"

2/25 - Some people who sell things on the train
(train: surabaja → bandung, java, indonesia)

Most of the world depends on rail travel to get from place to place. Trains (and their stations) quickly become floating cities, where it's easy to procure anything if you sit in the same seat long enough.

2/26-tourists try to figure out what they are eating (Jakarta, java, indonesia)

Guidebooks were tricky things, particularly as every backpacker at the time depended on the Lonely Planet series. On the one hand the historical essays and cultural advice were useful, but any place highly recommended was sure to be overcrowded with "Travelers." After a few months, I discovered that doing the opposite of what the books advised allowed me more interesting experiences.

2/27 - what i look like to indonesians (jakarta, java, indonesia)

By now I longed to step outside somewhere or hop on a bus without being inundated with sales pitches. Tall, white, and obviously Yankee, I felt like a hounded celebrity. Normal pleasures such as taking a walk in a park weren't always worth the hassle.

2/28- airport paranoia
(Hong Kong)

A modern airport was supremely disorienting. Also, it had been so long since I'd been separated from my bag, I felt naked without it on my back.

NAGRASI
TANJUNG
VISIT WITHOUT VISA
20 JAN 1991
VALID FOR TWO MONTHS
FROM THE DATE

IMMIGRATION
DEPARTED
20 JAN 1991
S
SINGAPORE

17 JAN 1991
LUAR

MALAYSIA IMMIGRATION
Padang Besar
SOCIAL/BUSINESS VISIT PASS
Reg. 11, Imm. Regs. 63
- 3 JAN 1991
Permitted to enter and remain
in West Malaysia and Sabah
for THREE MONTHS from
the date shown above.
- 2 APR 1991

27 NOV 1990
ADMITTED UNTIL 2 5 JAN 1991

IMMIGRATION
SERVICE
- 4 MAR 1991
DEPARTED
(3467)
HONG KONG

IMMIGRATION
SERVICE
- 2 APR 1991
(1748)
HONG KONG

Visitor permitted to remain
until
2 8 MAR 1991

IMMIGRATION
SERVICE
28 FEB 1991
HONG KONG

3/1- lady & her battery
bunnies (hong kong)

The street vendors I was accustomed to sold food grown in their gardens, not battery-operated toys.

3/2- casual wear (hong kong)

I went from being seen as an easy source of cash in Indonesia to looking like a bum in Hong Kong.

313 - high seas on expats' boat party (hong kong)

I managed to hook up with a group of British bankers (friends of a guy I met in Nepal when I bumped into another pal I'd traveled with in Egypt) who generously ignored my well-traveled odors and invited me to hang with them. Well aware that they were witnesses to the last gasp of Imperial Glory, these jolly expats enjoyed Hong Kong to the fullest, including renting out the occasional junk and boating out to some remote island for a spectacular lunch.

3/4- drinking games
(guangzhou, guangdong, china)

On my first night in China proper I sat down in a small outdoor café for dinner. Suddenly, a gaggle of friendly, alcohol-lubricated Chinese merchant marines at the next table insisted I join them for a cross-cultural marathon session of drinking games. Their game appeared simple at first: two opponents simultaneously thrust forward any number of fingers while loudly guessing the sum of the two hands (for example: If I throw out two fingers and you throw out three fingers *while* I yell, "five!"— I've won and you have to drink). These guys were champs, and played their game at such a blinding pace, that soon I was practically under the table. As a desperate measure, I introduced them to "quarters," hoping I would have the edge (China has no coin currency, even the smallest denominations are paper). Unfortunately, my new comrades picked it up quickly, which was bad news for my liver.

3/5- Shock. I am bitten by a pickpocket in a train station (guangzho, guangdong, china)

Chinese train stations were filled with huge crowds waiting in interminable lines to buy scarce tickets. As a Westerner, I had to procure "visitors" tickets (Theoretical shorter line, guaranteed higher price!) which had to be purchased from a special unmarked agent. As I stumbled from line to line looking for the correct line, I felt the telltale touch of light fingers digging for my wallet. Not light enough; I grabbed my wallet before the pickpocket did, then foolishly chased the would-be thief. After several minutes of hide-and-seek, I finally caught the guy. Suddenly, I realized I had no idea what to do next. Like a game of tag, I just assumed the jig was up. But the pickpocket, well aware of the harsh Chinese justice system, changed the rules and gave my hand a big chomp. The teeth marks remained for a week.

3/6-Young pioneers off to sweep the streets
(guangzhou, guangdong, china)

As the train seemed like too much bother, I decided to explore Guangzhou a bit more. Directly abutting Hong Kong and a newly minted free economic zone, the town was exploding into a big, post-communist, commercial metropolis. But old habits die hard and the patriotic communist youth corps were everywhere in town.

3/7- choosing what's for dinner (market, guangzhou, guangdong, china)

Actually, it was the fish market that gave me the heebie-jeebies. Eels were dispatched with frighteningly nonchalant accuracy and the gutters ran deep with their blood.

3/8- australian of chinese descent confuses locals
(wuzho, guangxi, china)

With China becoming an easier place to visit, many second- and third-generation Chinese immigrants were experiencing their "homeland" for the first time. But just because someone is racially similar doesn't mean they have much in common culturally.

3/9-trying to figure out the Café scene (Yangshuo, guangxi, china)

While many backpackers pretended that they left only their footprints when visiting remote locations, every town written up in Lonely Planet was quickly transformed by hordes of scruffy kids with wallets hanging around their necks stuffed with Western currency. Today I suspect that, outside of North Korea, few places can escape the backpackers hankering for banana pancakes and cafés.

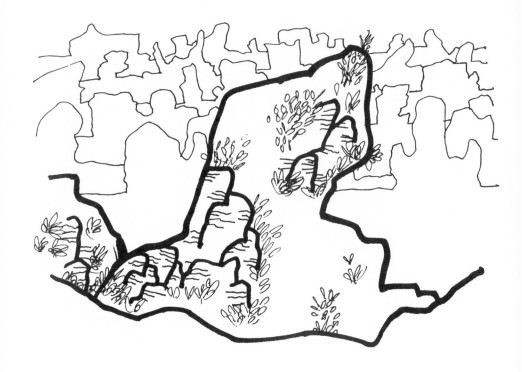

3/10 - a view from moon hill
(near yangshuo, guangxi, china)

I'd always admired Chinese ink scrolls with their expressionistic craggy mountains and misty vistas. So, I was unprepared to discover that they were barely stylized at all; the mountains of Guangxi really are as eerie and magnificent as their paintings. Thanks to Mao, the path leading to this stunning sight is called "Nixon Way."

314

3/11-workers work on workers' monument (yangshuo, guangxi, China)

Like Soviet Russia, China was filled to overflowing with grand statuary. To Western eyes it seemed oppressive, but the locals simply ignored the statues (much like we ignore all the advertising billboards littering our streets and highways).

3|12-blind man sees future (yangshuo, guangxi, China)

Communism, free-marketism, or whatever new -ism takes over the Chinese elite, there's always a place for folk fortune-tellers.

3/13 - salesman of rat poison & rat tails shows his wares (yangshuo, guangxi, China)

Of all the traveling salesmen I encountered on my trip, this guy had the best shtick and the greatest props. Judging by his clothes and haircut, he earned a pretty penny as well.

3/14- boarding a train
(train: every station, Guilin, guangxi →
shanghai, china)

Midtown subway rush hour has nothing on the Chinese trains, and having an Exalted Guest ticket didn't help in the push to get in.

3/15 - either wants to practice his english, or trade on the black market (shanghai - the bund - China)

Hanging out with guys who wanted to practice their English could be great fun. One guy I met, who took several minutes between each question to be certain he was picking the right words, tried to begin each sentence casually with a slow, deliberate, "By. The. Way . . ."

3/16 – tai chi (people's park, shanghai, china)

The town's main park was a racetrack before the revolution, but the anti-elite communist revolution transformed it into an idyllic park like New York City's Central Park with one exception: they charge admission to get in.

3/17 – child bundled up for the cold contemplates how he'll manage to walk with all those layers on (shanghai, china)

Cute as a button, wobbly as a Weeble.

3/18- posing (Qufu, Shandong, China)

The birthplace of Confucius, Qufu attracted Chinese visitors but few Westerners. With the exception of the various temples, monuments, and estates related to Confucius and his family, the town was unremarkable, which made it a fascinating opportunity to see normal Chinese life.

The local hostel was comprised of rooms in the Confucian clan's historic guest compound. Far from desiring "superiority," I just wanted to know where the toilets were.

3/20 - offering a cigarette
(tRAIN: Qufu → Beijing, china)

Long train rides could involve unnerving hours of being stared at, so I quickly learned to try and break the ice. Not that it always worked.

3/21 - they come from the hills
to sell medicinal deer bone
(Beijing, china)

Amidst the hustle and bustle, the smoke-belching buses and massive
construction projects, elements of Beijing seemed trapped in time.

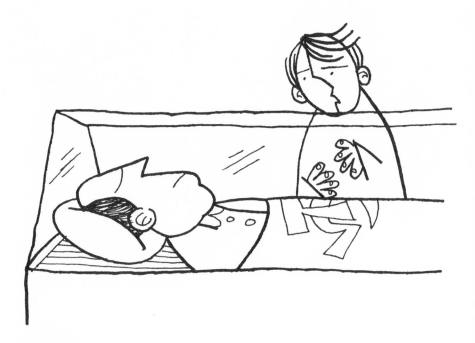

3/22 — one on one with mao
(Beijing, China)

I'd seen Lenin in Red Square, and I have to say that Mao was the more impressively preserved revolutionary leader.

3/23 - man applauds peacock's
plumage (beijing Zoo, China)

Life's simple pleasures.

3/24 - intercultural exchange at the railway station (beijing, China)

My new Swiss pal usually got his way without paying a bribe.

3/25-havin' hotpot in hohhot
(hohhot, inner mongolia, china)

Finding a sanctioned place to sleep in the capital of Inner Mongolia proved difficult, but eventually some buddies and I convinced a local official to allow us a night in the government dormitory, where four of us had the meal of our lives.

3/26 - the snow comes, the work stops, the snowball fights start (hohhot, inner mongolia, china)

Fun as it was, the blizzard meant that a visit to the Mongolian steppes and a week in a yurt was out. The weather up there could be severe; on the train ride up from Beijing I noticed villages where the wind came from the same direction so consistently that every building placed their entrance downwind.

3/27 - old kite flyer & fan
(Tiananmen Sq, beijing, China)

As it happened, I'd visited Tiananmen Square on a University trip in 1989, only a few months before an unsuccessful democratic revolt had transformed Beijing's center into a symbol of repression. Now, only a few years later, the square had returned to being the city's premier kite flying location (albeit with larger police presence).

3/28 - train station food vendor
(train: beijing → guangzhou, guangdong, china)

This was the beginning of a 44-hour train ride shmooshed up on a hard wooden bench as I descended from northern China back to Hong Kong. I could either eat what this woman had to offer or lean out the window at one of the stops to purchase something from a local vendor. Disposing of my empty containers was depressingly easy: everyone simply tossed their trash out the windows of the moving train.

3/29- sleeping on the train
(train: beijing → guangzhou, guangdong,
china)

This was the middle of the same train ride.

3/30 - dentist's storefront surgery
(Guangzhou, guangdong, china)

Taking the idea of a new openness to extremes.

3/31- Sunday morning gamble
(Macao)

The tiny territory of Macao was still a Portuguese colony in '91, a mishmash of romantic European villages and crass casinos. The gamblers took to their work with dull, bureaucrat-like seriousness; this was not the world of James Bond.

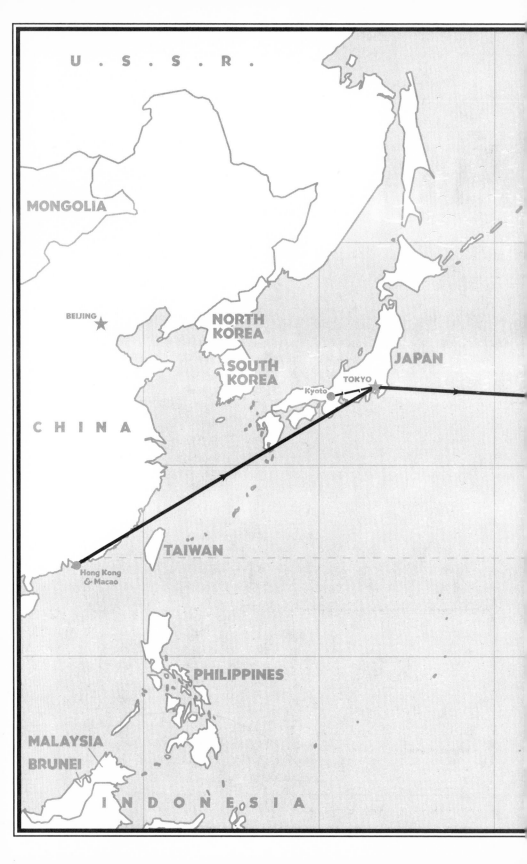

C A N A D A

U . S . A .

San Francisco

Big Sur

Las Vegas

Gallup

Flagstaff

Los Angeles

San Diego

Truth or Consequences

Austin

New Orleans

M E X I C O

BELIZE

GUATEMALA

EL SALVADOR

NICARAGUA

APRIL 1991

**Macao
Hong Kong
Japan
United States**

plane travel

car travel

hitchhiking

4/2— fortune-teller with his press clippings (Macao)

And that didn't include the clippings he knew he'd get in the future.

4/2 - busy, important people
(Hong Kong)

Cell phones were still new to me. The only time I'd previously seen a bunch of people walking around and talking to themselves was on Manhattan's Lower East Side. Note how big those phones look now.

43 – mahjong marathon
(Lantau Isle, Hong Kong)

With a quick ferry ride from the densely urban Hong Kong you could visit quaint beachy fishing villages where children collected shells and locals gambled outside.

SUBWAY MAP:

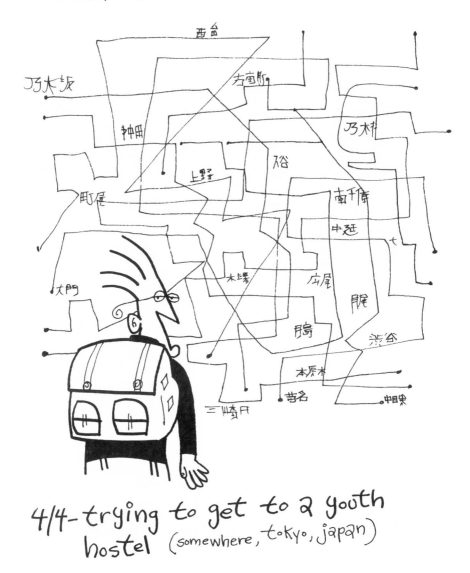

4/4-trying to get to a youth
hostel (somewhere, tokyo, japan)

Even after ten months of travel, I'd never been so confused about how to get from place A to place B as I was arriving in Tokyo. Each train or subway line is an independent concern, so transferring from one line to another is nearly impossible. The cost was also a shock. I spent more money getting from the airport to the youth hostel and buying a packet of cheese and crackers than I'd spent in the previous week.

415—they call them "love hotels"
(hitching: tokyo → Kyoto, japan)

Part Disney, part Reno, roadside Love Motels are windowless fantasy castles with convenient hourly rates and receptionists who apparently work behind opaque blinders, so as not to accidentally see any of the clientele. For all the effort put into these affair emporiums that dotted the landscape, parking one's car outside seemed to render all that discretion moot.

4/6-having a cup o' pure holy water (Kiyomizu temple, Kyoto, Japan)

I found Kyoto to be a beautiful and very walkable town (which was important on my budget). Although the stunning wooden temples claim great age, they were actually more recent replicas, as the originals had the tendency to burn down every century or so.

4/7 - shinto priest steals a
smoke before the tourists
start pouring in (Yasaka Shrine,
Kyoto, Japan)

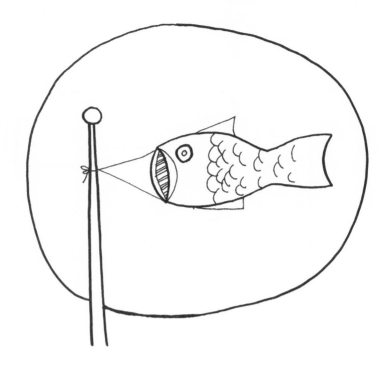

4/8 - fish kites for upcoming boys day festival (—Hitching: Kyoto → Tokyo, japan)

Hitchhiking in Japan was a different experience than in Southeast Asia. Japanese had little tradition of hitching, so it was hard to get picked up. Once you were, however, the host (teen, trucker, or dad) felt obligated to take care of you and/or shower you with gifts. My most successful ride was in the back of a car packed to the brim with clay. The driver's wife was a potter like my father. With that in common, I soon discovered myself at the driver's Tokyo home enjoying a fantastic dinner. I left that evening with a simple mug (that I still use to hold my drawing pens) and a smile, as I struggled in vain to figure out which commuter train would return me to my hostel.

4/9-Vending machines, Vending machines, Vending machines (tokyo, japan)

In Japan there is nothing that cannot be vended. Tokyo's population sleeps soundly with the knowledge that they could go out anytime, night or day, to purchase beer and women's underwear.

4/10 – drunk under the cherry-
blossoms (tokyo, japan)

The Cherry Blossom Festival was a sight to behold. It featured picnickers who sat (or slept) in roped-off sections beneath the gently cascading blossoms as others promenaded and giggled at the silly drunks.

4/11- an hour before landing in california,
passengers join in with the
"aerobics in the air" video
(plane: tokyo, japan → los angeles, CA →
New orleans, LA, USA)

My jaw hit the floor when the plane's video screen came to life with an image of a pink-leotarded hottie and two buff men sitting in airplane seats. As the hottie squealed that it was time to "get pumping!" the lady sitting next to me gave me an annoyed nudge for not joining in. I looked out the airplane window; we'd just passed over California; technically I was back in America.

regular access to toilet paper.

the english language.

4/12-two things i realize i missed about america

(New orleans, LA, USA)

4/13 - crawfish fa' dinna'
(new orleans, La., USA)

Initially, I'd planned to take buses across America from Los Angeles, but my parents convinced me to return to their house in New Orleans for a few days before continuing my trip. They offered the use of my mother's car as incentive, but it was the crawfish that clinched the deal.

4/14 - fais do do (cajun dancing)
(tipatina's, new orleans, La., USA)

Even though I was revisiting my favorite local sites, I felt like a tourist. It was disconcerting for everything to be so familiar yet foreign.

4/15 - the conversation is incomplete without peeling the labels off the beer bottles (new orleans, La, USA)

I love the laziness of New Orleans. A Cajun once asked me how I could live in New York where no one will simply "pass the time" and I didn't have a good answer. Fifteen years ago, I felt that New Orleans would always be there waiting for me with a drink in one hand and some Mardi Gras beads in the other. After hurricane Katrina destroyed my hometown, I can only hope that the leisurely pace of life will be rebuilt along with the houses.

4/16 - three armadillos on the highway (new orleans, La ——➔ austin, Tx, USA)

It seems that armadillos evolved the unfortunate defense strategy of jumping when they feel threatened, so whenever a car approaches they hop to the perfect height for a good whack into the front grille.

4/17- While watching a circus monkey on t.v. (Rendezvous Lounge, Tx, USA)

Gotta love Texas.

4/18 - boy determined to get ketchup packet in mop bucket during "game time" at McDonald's birthday party (truth or consequences, NM, USA)

You'd think a town named after a game show would have better games.

4/19- I-40 Landscape
(gallup, NM → Flagstaff, AZ, USA)

As my car hurtled down the Southwestern highways at tremendous speeds, I felt perfectly still and happily alone. Well, the signs were a little distracting.

4/20 - two old friends in Vegas
(Las Vegas, Nv, USA)

I've never been much of gambler. Neither was the guy with the mustache.

4/21- Weddings always make me cry (Las Vegas, N.V., USA)

It amazed me that everything I'd heard about Las Vegas (the drive-thru wedding chapels, the rows and rows of seedy pawnshops next to brightly glaring casinos) was true. I've heard that it's become "family friendly" in the last decade and a half, which to my mind only adds another layer of weirdness.

4/22- future rock star on hollywood blvd. (Los Angeles, CA, USA)

Los Angeles was for me the opposite of Las Vegas; here none of the stereotypes worked. Instead of glamour, the whole town seemed like a strip mall with muffler shops and a few deluded wannabe rockers.

4/23-the regular & the waitress
(san diego, CA, USA)

I met two recently returned veterans of the first Iraq war at this restaurant. The stories they told me and their newfound admiration for Vietnam vets was enlightening, and became useful a few days later when I found myself in an abandoned school bus in the mountains (see 4/25).

4/24-express lane (Los Angeles, CA, USA

Traffic in Los Angeles would make residents of third world capitals feel right at home.

4/25 - papa discusses music,
life & his dogs in his
school bus/home (the hills of
big sur, CA, USA)

Having driven far too long on Route 1, I stopped off at a roadside bar/diner for a bite, which led to chatting with the locals, a beer, and the sudden realization that I was too exhausted to drive the additional 50 miles or so to the next motel. "Papa" invited me to his "house," a school bus on bricks hidden in the woods on a sheer cliff overlooking the ocean. The evening started out fine; he chatted about his Vietnam experiences and I related how the Iraq War vets I'd met in San Diego expressed great respect for what his generation had gone through. By now the two mangy dogs were jumping around knocking beers out of our hands, so they could claim them for their own. Then a neighbor (from another nearby abandoned school bus) popped by, and the conversation turned to various arrest stories, some of which were harrowing. Their hackles up, my two buddies started to get a crazed look in their eyes as they cursed various lady friends who'd turned them in to the authorities over the years. I slept in my car and left at dawn the following morning.

4/26-haight street: meeting place of past decades
(San Francisco, CA, USA)

Like every guy in his early twenties, I had a romantic view of Haight-Ashbury, the San Franciscan Bohemian epicenter. Unfortunately, it seemed like everyone in the district had read the same history books as I, and were stuck in some sort of farcical dramatic reenactment, like a hippie/beatnik version of Colonial Williamsburg—except these reenactors didn't take off their costumes at the end of their shift.

4/27 - roller-skate renter
(San Francisco, CA, USA)

The Rollerblade fad didn't make much sense in hilly SF.

4/28- ballad (SAN francisco, CA, USA)

Punk rockers are filled with an anger born of showing up for a ten o'clock open-mike slot and having to wait three hours before being allowed on stage, by which time even their friends have left.

4|29-goatees galore (San Francisco, (CA, USA))

Having been away from the States for nearly a year, I had missed a lot of cultural experiences: the importance of CNN during the war, *Seinfeld*, and the goatee fungus that swept the nation.

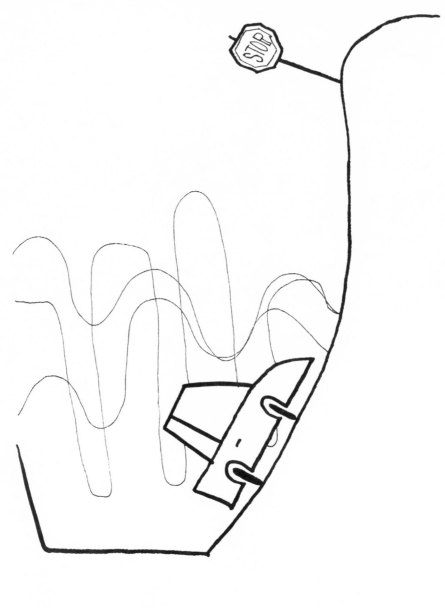

4/30 - driving (san francisco, CA, USA)

As Mark Twain once said, "Forget trying to parallel park in San Francisco; it's not worth it."

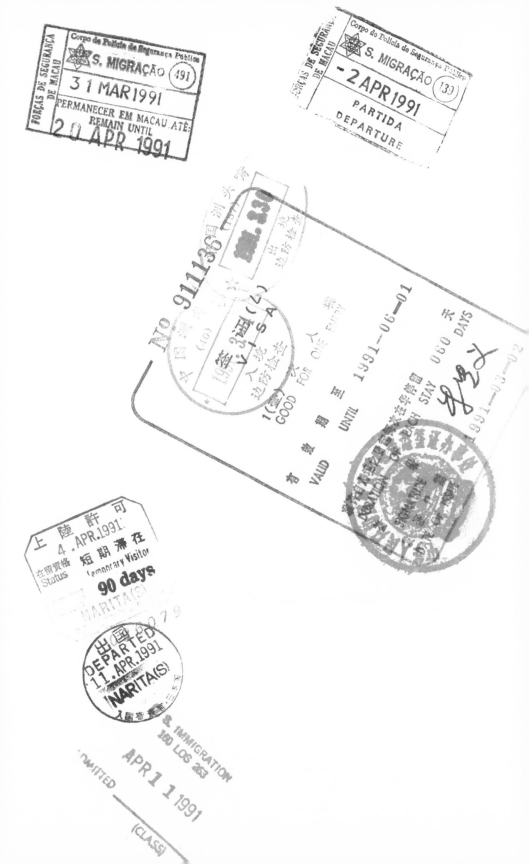

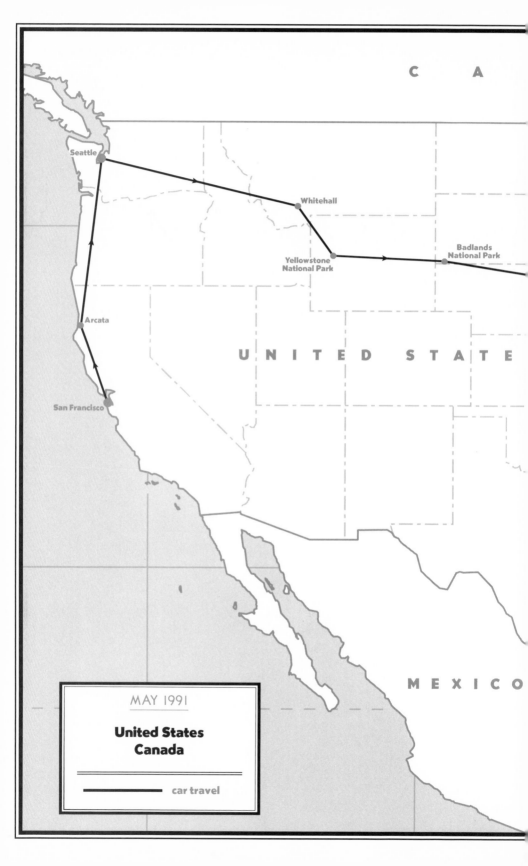

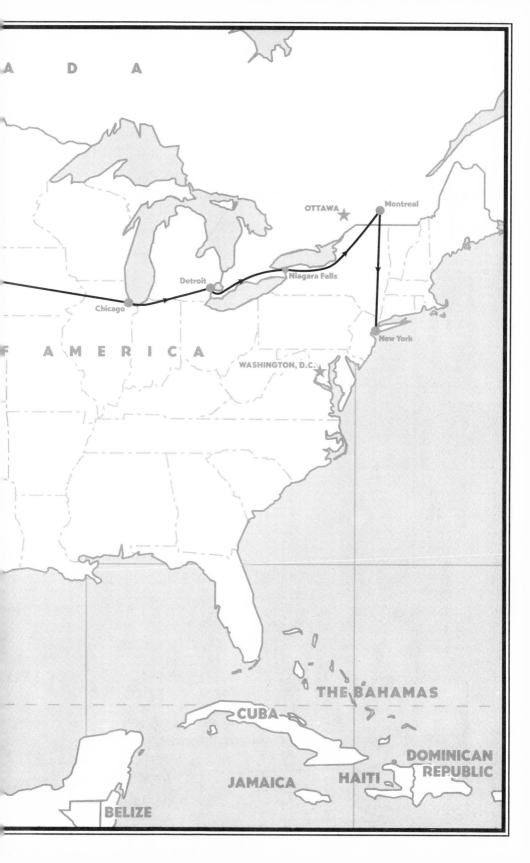

5/1- friends come over to look at surfer's photo book of great waves (near arcata, CA, USA)

I'd been given this guy's address from a friend of a friend of a friend. Having dedicated his life to surfing, he lived in a run-down shack on the beach, worked at menial jobs, and scanned the weather frequencies for wave opportunities. His passion for surfing gave us something in common: we'd both traveled around the world (he in search of the perfect wave). After a delicious repast of Leftover Squished Lentils in Unusual Sauce, his buddies and I sat around to look at his travel pictures, every single one of which was a blurry shot of a wave. His pals oohed and ahhed while I was reprimanded for turning the pages too quickly. After three albums of nearly identical photographs taken in Indonesia, Australia, and other romantic locales, I called it a night. The surfer dudes stayed up until dawn checking out the remaining stash of pictures.

5/2-redwoods (arcata, CA→
sattle, WA, USA)

Superman may be able to leap giant buildings, but he'd be hard pressed to bounce over a redwood.

5/3 - the museum (seattle, WA, USA)

By now I was such a sight, that no art exhibit could compete with me for sheer weirdness, as the kid staring at me (off panel) can attest. Unbeknownst to me, my eccentric hair, patched pants, and worldly odors would contribute to my upcoming ordeal in Detroit (see 5/14).

5/4-prelude to a pick-up
(seattle, WA, USA)

There's a law in Seattle that everyone must have their own sport. For this guy, it was chasin' tha ladies.

5/5 - fishmonger fun (seattle, WA, USA)

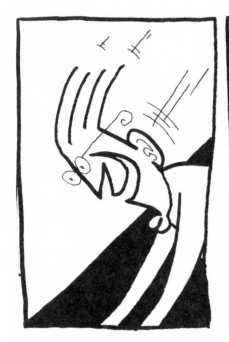

5/6 - biking downhill, biking uphill (Seattle, WA, USA)

Feeling guilty for not exercising in Seattle, I tried cycling. All in all it wasn't so bad, but had I stayed two days longer they would have made me buy a wet suit.

5/7 -tumbleweed (seattle, WA → Whitehall, MT, USA)

The constant, endless nothingness of Montana blew me away. No matter how fast I drove, it felt like the car was standing completely still.

5/8 - buffalo in snow (Yellowstone National Park, WY, USA)

Having been raised in New Orleans, I was unused to vast expanses of snow, particularly in May.

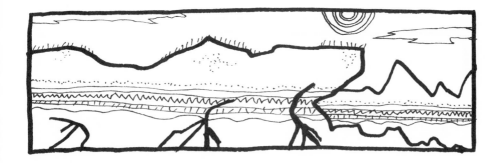

5/9 - the beautiful bad land
(badlands National park, SD, USA)

When I was about seven or eight my family rented a gigantic Winnebago and drove around the Badlands. Even then, the colors and shapes rocked my world. This time, I felt as if I'd be engulfed in a gigantic Paul Klee drawing. I would not experience colors like that again until I visited Tunisia in 1993.

5/10 – gosh. (the I-90, SD, USA)

At about a third the price of run-down motels, truck stops have the cheapest beds on the road. The catch: you have to be a trucker. I'm not dumb enough to pretend that my trucker imitation fooled anyone, but it was amusing enough to occasionally find myself enjoying dormitory accommodations and free, endless reruns of motocross racing on the "living room" TV. While most of the real truckers politely ignored me, I'd occasionally meet a chatty guy trying to get in on the same deal.

5/11 – the college girl
& her iguana
(chicago, IL, USA)

In Chicago I stayed with a young woman I'd met the year before while on a college trip to Russia. We had a ball in Moscow running around and generally raising hell, but in the Windy City the highlight was hanging with her pal's reptile.

5/12- regulars discuss sports,
politics, & spring gardening
plans (chicago, IL, USA)

5/13 - restaurant owner's child runs amok with a golf club during the entrée (chicago, IL, USA)

I have no memory of this, but it sure seems scary.

5/14—refused entry to CANADA
by inspector #1508
(Detroit, MI, USA)

Inspector #1508 had the steel-trap mind of a paranoid Inspector Clouseau. Furious that someone would attempt to cross the border during her coffee break, she regarded my passport with instant suspicion and declared that it had too many stamps on it—proof I was a drug runner. She took a peek at my vehicle, which had diplomatic plates (number 13 no less). My hair was too long to be a diplomat's, yet I claimed the car was my mother's—proof I was a car thief. I had only about 40 bucks on hand and my ATM and credit cards were obviously stolen (from someone with my exact name, no less!).

My big mistake, after 25 minutes of abuse, was to ask for a manager. Just for that, Inspector #1508 typed in her computer her conclusion that I was a wanted criminal. I had crossed the borders of Greece and Turkey, Israel and Egypt, and Pakistan and India, but this woman would be damned if I could get into Canada for a weekend. Giving up, I got in my "stolen" car and returned to America. The U.S. border guards laughed knowingly when I told them my tale. Inspector #1508 was famous.

5/15 - a difficult temptation to resist (niagara falls, NY, USA)

I also had this strange desire to get married. . . .

5/16 - application for a
Canadian tourist visa, II
(niagara falls, NY, USA)

Avoiding Inspector #1508's domain, I tried to get to Canada again, this time via Niagara Falls. Unfortunately, I hadn't really believed Inspector #1508 had posted a bulletin on the Canadian computer system describing me as fugitive drug runner. She had. Instantly, I was interrogated by an intimidating, gruff inspector. Gruff, but no dummy. I was obviously too incompetent and nervous to smuggle chewing gum. Still, my car was torn apart; the people I planned to visit were forced to fax paperwork accepting full legal responsibility for my actions during my stay; and if I remained in Canada one minute longer than my provisional visa allowed, I would be arrested. My cage rattled, I was released a few hours later and given a cheerful "Welcome to Canada!" brochure.

5/17_ the tourist's tourist
(montreal, CANADA)

All that for a rainy weekend in Montreal.

5/18 - whilst the band tries to play (MONTREAL, quebec, CANADA)

And this.

5/19 - after walking the dog, owner helps it back up to the 4th floor apartment
(New york, NY, USA)

So much for Canada; after 11 months and three weeks, I was desperate to return to someplace I knew. While New York City hadn't changed much in the intervening year, I had. I could only relate to the city in terms of my traveling experiences: 14th Street felt like New Delhi; the West Side Highway like Bangkok; the West Village like Malaysia's Georgetown. The plan was to spend a few days with friends and see New York from the outside, but I couldn't help flashing back on the past year in weird ways. That still doesn't explain why I drew someone dragging their dog up a flight of stairs. . . .

5/20 - houston st. phones
(New York, NY, USA)

I'd seen junked, rusted trash throughout the big trip, but never anything busted just for the fun of it.

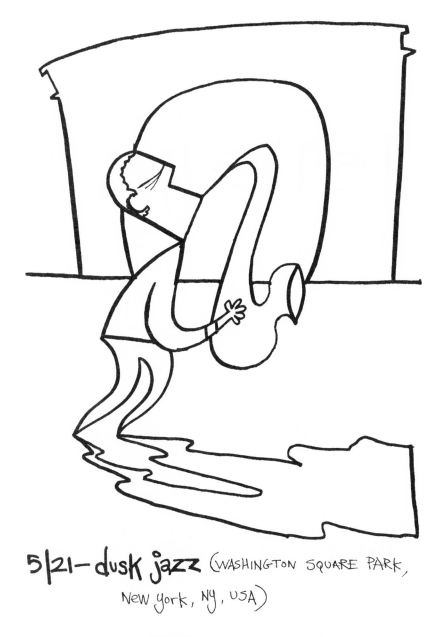

5/21—dusk jazz (WASHINGTON SQUARE PARK, NEW YORK, NY, USA)

Okay, here's a good rule of thumb: once you start making drawings of saxophone players in Washington Square Park, it's time to quit. That's exactly what I did. Ten days short of a full year, I packed my notebooks, dumped them in the trunk of my mother's car, and spent the next few days driving down to New Orleans, where I slept for a week before starting my adult life.

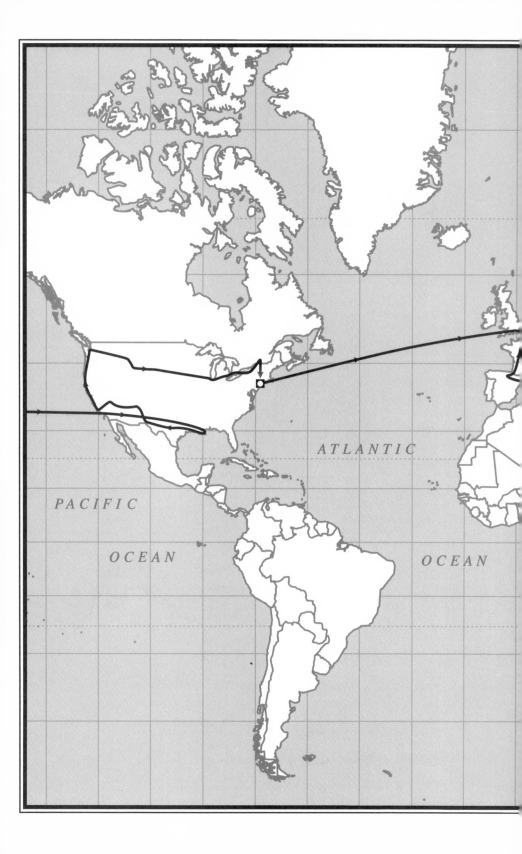

ATLANTIC

PACIFIC

OCEAN

OCEAN

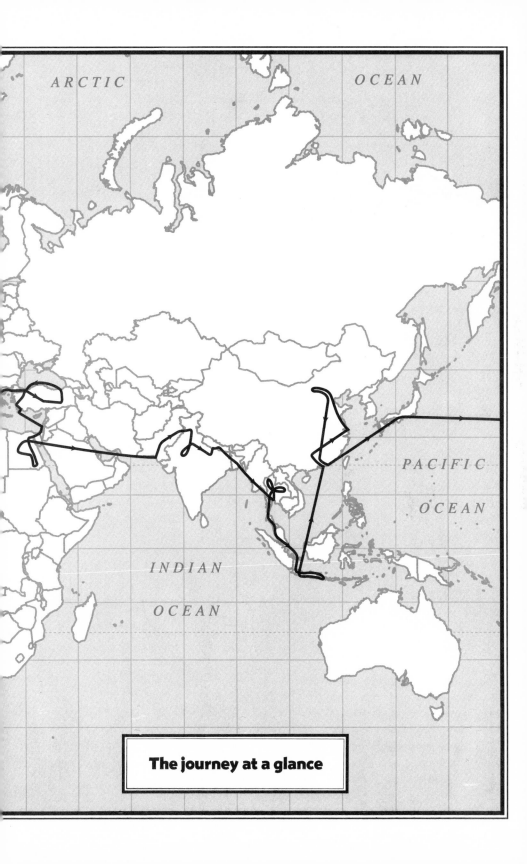

The journey at a glance

EPILOGUE

I'm no Marco Polo, Ibn Battuta, or Sir Richard Burton. I didn't return from the wilderness with all the answers. The world remains just as confusing and contradictory to me as it was before I visited it, if not more so.

Except now, having been there, I know the world isn't just a bunch of images that flicker on the TV whenever there's a natural disaster or riot or war. Those people that you hear about out there in those countries with the funny names, those people with their different clothes and ideas and facial hair—those people are *real*. They have families. And hopes. They're kind and cruel. Some admire America, some hate us. Some are very, very poor, others obscenely wealthy. But they all really exist, and what they do affects us.

I feel lucky (and sometimes guilty) to live in a country filled with both material wealth and a wealth of opinions. But to have had the opportunity to see and smell and partake in this big planet's profound weirdness has been, for me, the luckiest thing of all.

Now, those same people who said it was a small world also claim that you can never go home. Wrong again. After a summer sleeping in New Orleans, I returned to New York, where over the next decade and a half I found work, found a wife, and started a family; in short, I made a home.

Still, whenever I want to roam free and experience the world again, all I have to do is open my front door and step outside. I know that the world will be there to meet me. The same goes for you. I hope that one day you'll take the opportunity to put your life on hold and step out that door into this big, wide, wonderful world. It's a nice place to visit.